The Unexpected Pond

Editor Chris Firth

route

First Published in 2000 by Route
School Lane, Glasshoughton, West Yorks, WF10 4QH
e-mail: books@route-online.com

ISBN: 1 901927 05 9

Editor: Chris Firth
Cover Design: Andy Campbell
Cover Image: Henryk T Kaiser
Support: Ian Daley, Clayton Devanny, Nicole Devlin, Lorna Hey, Dean Smith,
Rachel Van Riel

Printed by Cox and Wyman, Reading

A catalogue for this book is available from the British Library

Full details of the Route programme of books
and live events can be found on our website
www.route-online.com

Route is the fiction imprint of YAC, a registered charity No 1007443

YAC is supported by

Contents

Introduction

Chris Firth

At one point in his 'career' the American psychopath, Charles Manson, would break into 'homes' with other members of his Family, simply to rearrange the furniture. The Family would reorganise the room, swap the pictures around, daub 'GETTING THE FEAR' on the walls, then go. Nothing taken. Nothing broken. Nobody butchered. Not until later. Imagine that feeling then, welling in your bowels and gut, when you came home, opened the door, were baffled by the room and read those words, scrawled in red, on your own walls. Imagine the paranoia later on, when you found out who had written these words, and what butchering they had done. Imagine the relief!

A few years ago a friend of mine came home from holiday to a similar, though less drastic experience. Her back door had been kicked open, bootprint still visible beside the shattered lock. Groans. Dropping bags. That gut-lurching sensation as she stepped through the door, expecting mayhem, or house emptied of contents. But everything was as normal. The drawers had not been ransacked. The TV and sound system were still on their racks. Nothing seemed to have been taken or disturbed. She rushed from room to room, so relieved that nothing was missing or broken. Then she went to switch the kitchen light on. No light. Looking up, no light bulb. And in every room it was the same. No lightbulbs. Not even in the bedside lamp. Every single bulb in the house had been 'stolen'. Of course, she reported it to the police but they could offer no reason for the crime.

Back a few more years now, and through a more aesthetical form of this kind of macabre intrusion, the Unexpected Pond Company was briefly formed - though with no intention or intellectual analysis about it at the time. Every Sunday afternoon at The Unmentionable Hotel (a once brilliant but now drab pub in Manningham, Bradford) a cluster of psychedelamphetaminhol bedazzled hangovers would meet for a few pints of ale to de-fragmentalise their comedowns. Inevitably the table-gibbering verged on the bizarre, and there was usually a lot of laughter. The pub has a beautiful beer-garden, and at one of these gatherings someone suggested that they should dig a fish pond in the middle of the lawn. Everybody nodded, smiled and agreed, and really that should have been it. But the idea was picked upon and turned over with disturbing singularity for weeks afterward. Tools were discussed; linings debated; time structures from first turf disturbance to the last drop of water considered. The Unexpected Pond Company had happenchancely been created. A month later, after an overnight SAS style operation, the pub had its unwanted and unexpected pond. Ponds became the company's collective obsession. At least half a dozen 'unexpected ponds' cropped up in gardens around the city over the next two months. Then the idea evaporated, bubbling away just as quickly as it had emerged, some other source of obsessional conversation shimmering through The Pond Company's Sunday ramblings.

The Unexpected Pond Company is long disbanded, but an ideology remains. How much more beautiful than red words daubed on walls; how much more aesthetically pleasing than removing lightbulbs - an unexpected pond.

Ponds - there's something slippery-beautiful, sinister, pleasing and mysterious about them. The still or breeze-rippled surface; green mist water; bulrushes and willowherb reflected in the luring mirror; the dangerous entangling weed and floating lily; the fascinating life swirls systemising within. Then the childhood tales of drownings and swollen corpses that everyone of us has heard. So, the strained but appropriate metaphor. A pond. A story. Everybody has their own.

On occasion, when sifting through the manuscripts submitted for this collection, I would read my way into something breathtaking, mysterious, exhilarating and beautiful. Not necessarily brilliantly written - not manicured and fenced off like a suburban garden pond - but still wild, fascinating, disturbing even. I would have stumbled upon some 'unexpected pond'. Maybe sometimes in need of a clean or a tidy up, but usually best left sinister and slightly neglected, crisp packets and coke cans still tangled in the weed beds, mythical bloated corpse just bobbling out of sight beneath the still surface.

So, that's how the title for this book came about. Now for the stories. No comment is really needed about these - let them speak for themselves. Immerse yourself, enjoy...

Diving

Julie Mellor

The sun was already starting to climb and the summer air was heavy with heat. Ricardo placed the bunch of red carnations in the shade behind the wall and adjusted the collar of his jacket. The flowers looked tired already; half open buds curling in the Sicilian sunshine.

In the distance was the ferry, grey against the solid blue of sea and the sky. People were gathering on the quayside to welcome it into port. Meeting the ferry was a sort of tradition here, like going to church on Sundays; it marked the passing of another week. Ricardo felt a bead of sweat tickle under his arm and run down his side. The suit he was wearing was a merino blend. Too heavy for summer but top quality, even if it was a little worn at the elbows. He felt the place where the cloth was thinnest and hoped Angelina wouldn't notice.

He held his breath. What if she wasn't on the boat? What if she'd changed her mind?

She was always saying she loved him in her letters, but writing about love wasn't the same as being with someone. Letters were distant things; the touch of paper wasn't the same as the touch of skin. She'd been two years in America. It was a long time. He tried to think of her face but found he couldn't. Instead he saw her heart, picturing it as a flower, a red carnation plucked from its stem and pressed flat to preserve it. Dry and lifeless, all the love squeezed out.

People pushed past him to get the best position on the quayside but Ricardo wasn't going to lose his dignity by pushing like a common animal. So what if he was out of work? That didn't make him any less of a man, did it? He smoothed his hands down his trousers. A perfect fit. The previous owner must have been his size exactly. Not often you got a second hand suit that fitted so well. He felt the jab of an elbow in his side as a woman pushed past him, followed by an old man leaning on a stick. Soon he was unable to see anything except the proud chimney of the ferry and the thick knot of smoke which rose from it.

The faraglione was a huge rough finger of rock that pointed up from the sea to mark the entrance to the harbour. The ferry had to slow to avoid it. As it reduced its speed the whirl of smoke became denser. In the push a little girl with melted chocolate on her fingers caught hold of Ricardo's hand, then proceeded to hug his leg and wipe her smeary face on his thigh. Ricardo tried to pull away but the pressure of the crowd kept the child glued to him. His suit! His new suit! He shook his hand to rid himself of her and she began to cry. A whimper at first, then a loud wail, cutting across the noise of the crowd and the low grumble of the ferry's engine. People started to look round and soon everyone was staring. Ricardo held up his hands to signal that he had done nothing wrong, but it only served to confirm his guilt.

Out of the mass of faces a woman with a wide brimmed hat stepped forward and snatched up the child. Away from Ricardo the little girl started to scream, 'Papa! Papa!' Ricardo didn't know what to do, what to say. He held up his hands again, shrugged his shoulders. Nothing to do with him. When he and Angelina had children they wouldn't behave like that. He scowled a sour-lemon face at the child, still wailing 'Papa, Papa.' People were looking at him. The suit made him feel conspicuous, as though the whole crowd knew he'd bought it second hand.

So what? Were they any better than him? Were they? His mouth opened and closed like a fish but no sound came. The woman tried to calm her daughter, kissed and petted her, held her close. 'Shush,' she said, 'Papa's dead.'

Dead? Ricardo swallowed. The suit seemed to shrink around him, tight like a second skin, suffocating. He looked down to avoid the angry stares that were coming from all points, and focused instead on the sticky brown handprint the child had daubed on his trousers. Dead? Keeping his head bent he moved away.

The blue sea dissolved to turquoise as the ship entered the

bay, disturbing the sand, making patterns in the water. The swirling colours looked so inviting. He wished he could ditch the suit and dive in. The desire brought back memories of his boyhood, of summers spent diving from the rocks. He looked towards the faraglione, its jagged face weathered by the constant smack of the waves, and remembered the sensation of falling through the air, of plunging into the deep blue underworld. He wondered whether Angelina would remember too.

He returned to the low wall where he had placed the flowers. Someone had trodden on the stems and they had split, revealing stringy green veins inside. A sap stain in the shape of a love heart marked the concrete. Ricardo sat down and removed the shoes he had borrowed from his brother. He wriggled his toes and felt the blood return. The relief was instant. Then he slipped off the jacket and placed it over the wall. It relaxed across the shape of the stone like someone laying down to sleep. Or to die, he thought. The child's voice rung in his head like a tolling bell, 'Papa! Papa!' He wondered who the man had been. Not poor like himself; the material was expensive and the cut was too good. He loosened his tie to get some air, pulled, and felt it slither around the back of his neck. It was then that he made the decision.

Everyone was too busy watching the ferry to care about him, but still, he turned his back to the crowd for the sake of modesty before he undid the buttons of his trousers. Then placing his clothes in a pile beside the trampled flowers, he walked quickly up the quay, away from the crowd to a couple of old men who sat with lines, watching the bob and dip of their floats.

'Buongiorno,' they saluted in unison, seemingly oblivious to the fact that all Ricardo was wearing was his baggy white underwear.

12

'Buongiorno,' replied Ricardo, shifting his weight from one foot to another on the hot concrete.

'Hey, don't disturb the fish,' complained one of the men.

'Scusa,' said Ricardo politely, and moved a little further away. The ferry was steadily approaching. He'd better hurry if he wanted Angelina to see. He looked back at the crowd and saw the woman and the child watching him. He wanted to explain. Say he was sorry. But it was too late for that. He regarded the water for a moment longer, the ever changing pattern of the surface, the constant darkness below, then he pegged his nose between thumb and forefinger, and jumped.

Slick, liquid numbness touched every part of him, licking his ears, fingering between his toes, cold and intimate. He surfaced with a splash and blast, his head breaking the water, droplets scattering. And that was when he caught sight of her, leaning on the banister rail of the ferry like a figurehead. He screwed his eyes up and looked again. Was it really her?

Her hair, which had hung loose down her back, was now held off her face with a thick ribbon, and she was wearing a dress of bubble-gum pink with a nipped-in waist, falling to a full circle below her knees. When the wind caught it, it puffed and blew like a sail.

'Angelina, Angelina,' he cried, treading water and waving his arms, but the ship's engine was in reverse, noisily sucking back in order to slow down before docking. The water rumbled. What had possessed him to do this? He was practically a married man now. A poor one at that. He shouldn't be splashing about in the water like an idiot. But people were watching. It was too late to turn back.

The faraglione stood like a melted candle, rivulets of volcanic rock set down the side in strange petrified shapes. Ricardo swam as fast as he could, and when he reached the base he scrambled out, stopping for a moment to feel the casual warmth of sun on his skin. The rock was slippery from the constant wash of the sea, but he began to climb, and when he reached a little higher it became dry and easier to grip. The sun seemed to climb with him, further and further up, warm on his back, drying the hair at the nape of his neck. There were three or four good places from which to dive, but he was only interested in one; the highest. When he reached it he turned and waved. He saw Angelina lift her hand half way, hesitating, uncertain, then she lifted it high and waved back. His heart felt so light it bobbed like the fishermen's floats. A crowd of passengers stood beside her now on the deck, waiting for him to dive, as well as the people gathered on the quayside.

He didn't look down into the water, which was almost black from this height, but out to sea, to the distant hazy line of the horizon. A vast empty space begging to be discovered. What if she had changed her mind? It wasn't unheard of for girls to back out at the last minute. She'd been away so long. He wished he had more to offer her. What if love wasn't enough?

He crossed himself then drew a deep breath, drew in again deeper, and raised his arms to dive. The take off was straight and swift, the wind sounding like waves in his ears. He sped towards the water, or was it the water speeding towards him? At the precise moment before he hit the sea, he couldn't quite tell. Then he was in. The sensation was cool and sharp; the tang of salt stinging his eyes, the burst of trapped air escaping from his nostrils, bubbles giggling from his lips.

By widening his arms and arching his back he knew he could flatten his descent, but that wasn't what he wanted. He wanted to impress Angelina, and the crowd. To do that, he had to go deep. He released two gulps of air. They expanded in the water, rainbow-coloured like soap bubbles, straining for space against the weight of the sea, revolving like little worlds as they rose.

He quelled the reflex to take in air and made his insides stretch to hold his breath. He swam as deep as possible, down into the darkness, taking great armfuls of water in big wide strokes as he pulled himself towards the bottom. Timid fish darted, striped fins and glassy unblinking eyes. Deeper and deeper he went until at last he was on the sea bed, touching the sand, brushing it so that it clouded up around him like a storm; a fog of silica grains. And out of it another eye met his.

At first he thought it was a fish, but as the mist cleared he saw that it was a human eye with a fine arched brow, painted onto a fragment of pottery. He scrubbed the sea bed with his palm and found, beneath the sand, some pieces of a shattered vase. On the fragment in his hand he could make out the tightly curled hair and aquiline nose of a Greek woman, a goddess perhaps, immortalised on the terracotta. Two more bubbles escaped from his lips, spiralling desperately to the surface. His chest ached so much he thought it was about to split in two, but he couldn't go back now. Feather soft weed caressed the soles of his feet and sand swirled around his ankles, inviting him to stay.

Suddenly he felt a sharp jab as a piece of broken pottery caught his foot. A crimson ribbon weaved up through the sand and wrapped itself around his leg. The salt water made the wound smart and he opened his mouth instinctively to gasp. Immediately the sea pushed in, pressing down his throat, a great watery fist plunging into his mouth. He tried to cry out but he was voiceless, silenced by the weight of the sea. He reached up, grasping the last escaping air bubbles as they fled, but all his snatching was in vain because his limbs were becoming heavy, and his lungs flooding. Dizziness fizzed in his head like lemonade. It was all so quick, and although he struggled he couldn't do anything. The sea was winning.

He went limp, fell backwards, lay like drift wood and closed his eyes.

It was then that he realised he was still breathing, that although his lungs were full of water he was alive. Impossible. He became conscious of a strange tickling sensation at the side of his neck, like the beat of a pulse only stronger, more pronounced. He touched the spot with his hand and felt a small crescent-shaped muscle, opening and closing like a pouting mouth. The other side was the same. Gills! But he couldn't have gills. Could he? The dizziness was still there, prickling behind his eyes, but he was sure of it; he was breathing underwater. He wanted to shout out, but he couldn't make a sound because the water absorbed it. So he plunged and turned instead, somersaulted and spun until he had whipped up all the sand and couldn't tell which way was up and which way was down.

In the haze something fluttered. At first he mistook it for a shell but as he reached out to catch it he saw it was the piece of the broken vase which had first attracted him. A beautiful Greek woman, her eyes half smiling, as though she were about to tell him a secret. She floated just out of reach, spinning and darting, leading him across the sea bed, to a place where the sand was thin. When he scuffed it with his foot he saw that beneath him was a heap of vases and bowls, some ruined but others intact, cushioned by the weeds. He knelt down to take a better look. Half naked women reclining on couches, girlish boys with supple limbs. Some of the pieces were perfect.

Just then the sea began to darken. Ricardo looked up as the shadow of the ferry passed slowly and silently above his head, cutting out the reflection of the sun. Then came the propeller, a big flower twirling on its stem. He remembered the carnations, squashed and flattened. Angelina. She would be waiting. But he had nothing to give her. He reached out and took one of the vases, small and delicate, and began to swim to the surface, his white cotton underwear billowing as though it were drying on a line.

Surfacing was like slipping through silk, smooth and cool. Everything was so much brighter. He held his free hand to his eyes, kicking water to stay afloat, surprised at the dryness of the air as he took his first breath, the way it rasped his throat. His head was clear now. Tentatively he felt the side of his neck for the curved gills but the skin was quite firm and intact.

There was a shriek from the direction of the boat, then a series of whistles and shouts and clapping hands. So many people impressed by his dive, Angelina in the middle of them, waving her velvet ribbon.

He swam inelegantly, one hand holding the vase, the other paddling through the water. At the base of the faraglione he placed the vase carefully and scrambled up, sitting in the sun for a while to regain his strength. He could hear a child shouting and when he looked towards the quayside he saw the little girl waving at him too. Waving and smiling.

The ferry was weighing anchor. Soon the gang-plank would be lowered and people would fill the quayside. He would have to hurry. Angelina would be waiting. He picked up the vase and looked at it. Out of the water it seemed quite dull. He turned it over in his hands so the painted figures passed by, one after another, dragging their heels. Was it really his to give? Waves licked round the base of the rock. Bad enough that he had bought a dead man's suit. Did he want to be known as a thief as well?

He considered the vase for a moment longer, then threw it gently into the water. It sat for a second on the surface before it sank, a single bubble rising as it spiralled down to the place he had found it. Inside his chest he felt a sort of hollowness, but he dismissed it as just the freshness of air in his lungs.

Velvet Swamp

Rose Hughes

Once upon a time I lived in a tower on the edge of a crumbling estate. I stayed there all alone and ventured out once a fortnight to stock up on vegetables. I boiled them all in a pan I covered with a dustbin lid and I never went hungry. The pan was kept on a low simmer, and towards the tenth day or so I'd add whatever was at hand to the thick black mess to stretch it out. I seasoned my daily bowl according to which place in the world I happened to be thinking about that day; a dash of Tabasco if it was the Louisiana Swamps, or a feisty pinch of paprika if the sun was shining.

It got that I didn't know who or where I was after a time. I looked at my spice rack for clues and took an inventory of my furnishings to establish my gender. I had no visitors and lost myself more and more in strange books. My room smelt musty no matter how much I aired it. I counted the days off by the amount of tobacco I consumed; judging by the heap of butts blocking the door I must have been there a thousand years or more.

I was rotting: I had eczema all over me. My inside was like one of the used water filters I cracked open and lined up on my shelf as memento mori. Don't misunderstand me; I liked to let my hair down once in a while and bring in some company, somebody to tell me that the broth was gorgeous just as it was, but it always seemed to end in tears.

My last lover had a laugh like the peal of wedding bells. You could hear it far and wide, it drowned out the roadworks and the Council said that she had to go. I tried to let her down the way I like to be let down myself but living on the thirty-second floor it isn't always easy. The one before that made love to me with the finesse of a chicken sexer; she went too. The pile of casualties was beginning to resemble what lay behind my front door, and the postman wasn't happy.

The lift was my guide to any other human activity in the tower. On a good day it smelt of sweat, beer and urine. Sometimes it was like being trapped inside a bong. Weekends it was best avoided and I saved a stiff pair of boots for emergencies. By Monday morning the floor would always be mopped out and ready for action and if the lift got stuck you could ice skate until rescued. Once I found a row of canned pulses lined up in the gap where the coffins go, the sell-by date wasn't up so I kept them and feasted like a king that week.

From the balcony I could touch the sky with my fingers. Of a fine evening the rich blues and purples bled into each other, trickling down my arm. This was because of the pollution; pollution isn't all bad. Sometimes I'd sign my name like God must have done. I'd stand there and wave my arms in the air like a conductor. I'd get carried away and write messages to people in the other towers. Or stories. I'd babble away many an evening into thin air.

My imagination you see is quite vivid, even when I'm asleep. One night I dreamt that my father was lying on the ground like a fallen oak tree. On the soles of his feet it said DO NOT USE WITH SOAP. My mother was standing over him, distraught, shouting that she'd just given him a bath. Often I'd dream of digger trucks chasing me, and their crocodile smiles would unnerve me for days afterwards.

I had a recurring dream when I was a child. It was about a beautiful woman who'd sit on the edge of my bed and stare at me. She never spoke to me and it didn't occur to me to be afraid. She had a sad slow smile and the ache of it went right through me. Compared to her, most of my lovers never stood a chance.

I had a moat too, of sorts. There was a mound outside the main entrance down below with a sign to warn drivers to go slow lest they lose a clutch. At the bottom of it there was a permanent puddle and when the weather was bad I had my own private piranha pool to keep me safe. Only the brave, or the stupid, scudded in and out this way, or out-of-towners. Most took to the railings, even the infirm. Fresh roses often lay strewn on the grass verge beneath. One evening I was gathering some roses to brighten up my room when I heard a vehicle roar off into the distance. I looked up and noticed a dark figure slumped against the main door and I could see that she had a note pinned to her coat. On closer inspection it seemed to be written in hieroglyphics in an unsteady scrawl. I can turn my hand to most things and read out loud the message: 'She is my only daughter. Her name is Carmel. Please take care of her.' I couldn't see her face very clearly because her hood was up, but her skin was so pale it almost shone in the dark. Somehow I managed to get her up to where I lived. In the lift I noticed that she smelt of vomit and her icy grip on my wrist repulsed me. She put herself to bed in my box room and I spent the night on the balcony, chain-smoking.

The next few days passed quickly as I had to design a costume for the annual parade. I forgot all about my sleeping house guest. One year I went to the parade dressed in a bridal gown with a hundred-yard train. I had to lower myself down the side of the tower because I couldn't fit in the lift. I mingled so much that day, by evening I had all the revellers bunched behind me in a grubby white knot, so this time I was told to be less ambitious. I had a lover once who handcuffed herself to me and dragged me all the way to the parade. We were not let in on the celebrations, they told us we were considered a fire hazard.

I was sewing together the last few leaves of my cape when I noticed a slight breeze disturbing my artistry. Fearful for my ferny floor, I was just about to nail the windows shut when I felt a soft touch on my shoulder and a woman's voice said, 'I'll do it for you.' It was Carmel. I sat there in her slipstream and watched her perform the task as if she was playing a lazy game of shuttlecock on an English country lawn. I hadn't moisturised that day, so engrossed I was in my labour, and I furtively rubbed some elbow grease down my nose while her back was turned. If she heard a noise like the striking of a match she had the breeding not to flinch. When my new guest turned around I must have panted like a dog chasing a stick. She was beautiful.

That evening I found myself talking verse for the first time in years. The sonnets flew out of me and Carmel sat facing me amongst the foliage listening in silence. I conjured up plots for plays with ease, and at each fresh denouement she'd nod kindly in approval. Her own knowledge seemed inexhaustible; I'd talk about science or geography or ancient mythology, and she was able to clear up moot points that had never been clear to me before. She told me about events in history with such precision it was almost as if she'd been there. Of herself she revealed very little except that she had no issue, like myself, and that she was from a very rich family that went back many generations. I forgave her both this and her erudition simply because at times she seemed so sad and lost. She looked perturbed and far away and I wondered if the altitude bothered her. I don't remember going to bed that night, or the latter parts of our conversation. I slept like a Pisces and upon surfacing at noon the next day I found that my tongue had swollen slightly from my wild ramblings the night before. Or perhaps it was my latest piercing, who knows?

Carmel's mother never did come back to reclaim her and after a period I considered her mine. We fell into a routine of sorts, and I sometimes felt we lived in a weather house not a tower; I rose early, and tended to the rusted water tank all morning, but she never appeared before six or seven, by which time the water would be running clear as spring water. Her health had improved since that first night but she was often fatigued; she took baths until after midnight, and she always wore my dark bath robe as if to signal she didn't want to go out. So we stayed in most of the time. She'd ask me questions and I'd talk but once or twice I did lure her outside to ride about the estate with me. We must have cut a strange pair, my red face and her white.

Once we skinny-dipped in the moat. It was then that it struck me just how different we were. I'd dive off the railings and not come up for air until I'd retrieved a clutch from the murky depths while she floated on her back watching the moon. I must confess I felt slightly sacrilegious placing each rusted baton on her soft white belly as if it was a pearl, but she didn't complain. Her curly black hair anchored her still; I reached out for its tangled mess to guide me to the surface. I liked the way it tickled my cracked and bleeding skin. If on occasions I took too long, Carmel lazily scooped me up with her strong bony hands. I think I was happy down there, where the only sound was the muffled staccato of the road drills and the faint distant echo of towers collapsing. In the moonlight Carmel's hair was like a huge obsidian mirror and I felt I could have drifted forever in our velvet swamp, if I ever had the choice.

I dreamt around then that we were in a thermal pool in Budapest. Sulphuric fumes rose into the air and Carmel looked at home. Then we were in the cold plunge pool. It was announced in a foreign tongue, which baffled me, that the wave machine was about to be switched on. When the tidal wave approached I screamed, thinking that there was an earthquake, but Carmel just stepped out of the pool, cool as ice.

She never seemed to eat very much; conversation sated her. It was Carmel who changed my dietary habits for once and for all; even now I can't eat vegetables. She told me about nature's treasures; about royal peppers, tropical avocado, enchanted broccoli, great whale aubergine, until I was dizzy with anticipation. Once a fortnight I was in heaven and the lean days in between were a small price to pay. It gave me something to look forward to, and one by one the spices went out the window. I took to finger salt instead which Carmel would serve me in a tiny china bowl.

One evening we were out on the balcony looking at the sky and sharing a fat Havana cigar I'd found, when Carmel started on her now predictable interrogation, except this time she asked me to talk of my past lovers, a subject I'd been dreading. At first I was slightly repulsed by her strange androgynous features, but of late I'd found myself thinking about her when I was reading, and I'd silently stand outside her door while she slept. So I started with the most recent, and how her laugh had left me with tinnitus. I make things up sometimes when I'm nervous or I want to impress, and I could feel her intelligent eyes staring at me patiently. Her words when they came cut through the fug like a stiletto and I'll never forget them:

'Alone, alone, all, all alone
Alone on a wide, wide sea!
Never a Saint took pity on
— My soul in agony.'

After a lifetime I looked around but Carmel had gone. All that was left was her requiem voice echoing around the tower.

I must tell you that I made it to the parade that year. I got into trouble again, this time because my boots were so pointed I stabbed the leader of our procession in the back and it took twenty men to pull him off. People ran to join in thinking it was a tug-of-war, and he was almost ripped in two. Later he said it wasn't the pain that bothered him so much, it was the fact everybody knew before he did. He resembled an open zip for a long time, poor man, and all the young children from the estate would run around him teasing him cruelly.

This is either where my story starts or where it ends, I'm not too sure. Memory is a slippery, slippery eel. I used to believe that the past was a pagan theatre, just like my dreams, a series of pictures that could be made sense of like the note I found on Carmel the first time we met. But how can you ever fully recall what took place in the dark if you had your eyes shut most of the time?

Diabolis Necrolatry

Zenko Zdolyny

This book must have blood, and that is its Law...

Thus runs the first line of ***Diabolis Necrolatry***, whatever casual or cursory page the dark volume is flipped open upon.

Although familiar with the lore and fabled history of the book, Theo Faulkner sniggered at the absurd, melodramatic line after thumbing his copy open. Bespectacled, balding, slight and sneery, possessing a keen intelligence, Faulkner was a hero of the intellect, at least in his own imaginings. Speed, strength, physical courage - these qualities meant little to him. He considered himself an adventurer upon the battlefields and bad-lands of the human mind. A thinker, rather than a doer, believing that whatever new ideas he could come up with alone would reoccur in the species as a whole, much like an innovative rat in those psychological experiments - one who initially works its way through a prepared maze, thus enabling its fellows to follow its trials and errors through some inexplicable psychic link. There was no place or need, in his reasoning, for the barbaric, weapon-wielding champions of old. All his heroes - Einstein, Hawkins, Kafka, Nietzsche - had used pure mind and rational thought to attain their victories. The very reading of the *Necrolatry*, decoding a damned and cursed text, was for Faulkner *the* heroic deed. But as he skimmed past the opening sentence his courage faltered. The superior sneer faded. His knuckles whitened against the black leather cover as his hands began to tremble. He would have dashed the unholy object to the floor, but out of compulsive curiosity, and due to the nature of the curse, he could not. Within a paragraph it was his own life that was snaking there upon the yellowed page. Intimate, dark and secret incidents from his own experience unfolded in print before his eyes - details that could not have been written there by chance alone a century ago. The words came swimming up toward him from the page, worming their way through the space between his eyes and the paper. With an actual, painful throb of his heart he realised this meant that the myths were true. He tried to avert his eyes, to undo the opening of the voyage embarked upon but it was too late now. He was the book's plaything. The text would unfold him to the end. Though he tried to drag his mind away it was enslaved. He could not stop himself from completing the horrendous page....

*

In a corner of the gas lit basement the Black Sage scribbled furiously, generating a heat of words. As the ritual demanded, he used an old fashioned feather quill and wrote upon hempen paper. At last he was approaching something like an end to his great work. Around him was a fury of activity. Apprentices of The Order snatched up the finished, hand-scribed leaves, the ink still damp, passing them over to others whose task it was to set the words for the presses. Each letter, sign, mark and symbol had to be placed in the exact order the possessed Sage had scribed, whether the sentence or lettering of the word made sense or not. Logical order and rational sequence were irrelevant here, as they were destined to become in all Art. A moment is now. Now is past. The moment exists. Illogical rationality. He knew that there was no point in writing his book, but write it he must. So he scribbled and he scraped, possessed by Divine Fury. The book being thus born was the *Diabolis Necrolatry*, created by Maximus Cefalu, that infamous Black Sage, High Priest and High Fiend of The Golden Order Of The Brothers Of The New Dawn. The Great Tree from which, even as he wrote the line now, less disciplined, more dangerous offshoot Occult Churches were sprouting.

Twenty-five years previously, after an illuminated night of prophetic revelation, Cefalu had staggered upright in his cell and made a declaration to his devotees. Given the right circumstances, rituals, parchment, ink and binding, he could create a work of High Art that would perplex and baffle the human mind until the extinction of the species. He further announced that he was ordained to produce a work of fiction that would not remain fast upon the printed page; a work that would continually reform and rework itself upon the paper within its cover. In short, he would astound the world by producing a book that would perpetually rewrite itself.

Whether there was any merit in such a task Cefalu cared not, for the vision simply decreed that he must produce it - it was not his place within the hierarchy of The Order to question Divine Will.

Now, a quarter of a century later, after grinding poverty, bitter struggle, every kind of sneering mockery and ridicule from literary and theological circles, the circumstances were right. As he approached the last humanly constructed paragraph, chanting from the temple above the printing room rose to fever pitch. As his scribbles poured forth, he could hear strange, strangled shouts of blasphemy. He was writing faster and faster. A sense of feeling welled up in him not unlike, he wrote there, that excitement of approaching sexual orgasm - the welling of blood and senses that a rutting, lust-fuelled human male feels when copulating with a mate. Even as the sentence was down and drying, a woman shrieked in the room above. She whimpered, begged, implored for mercy - whether in ecstasy or pain he knew not. The chanting of the acolytes rose above her cries. The Sage was sure he heard the mewling of a new-born infant and this he wrote. Then all above was abrupt silence. His own pen scraped to a halt, mid-sentence, and an audible gasp escaped his lips. His whole body quivered. He had done. It was over.

'Aaahh!'

Le petit mort.

A final spasm of words.

He had finished.

The house and printing press was situated in a quiet terrace in Bloomsbury, London. Breaking the sudden silence that had pervaded the building, he heard the bells of St Martin's strike out midnight.

'This is done,' Cefalu croaked.

'Then is now. Is the press ready?'

A novice took the final sheet from his offering hand and hurried it across to the typesetters.

'Master, the press is ready. We now await the ink, and then we can begin.'

Three loud, singular knocks sounded upon the basement door. It opened. A bearded High Priest with long black coils of hair and the electric-green eyes of a tiger stepped into the room. His movements were feline also, fluid and stately. In one hand he held the carved, ebony staff of rank, a golden bowl cupped delicately in the other. Female acolytes with bedraggled hair and wild passion fuelled eyes filed in after their beloved Master. Without a word this fiend-priest, Crowley, for it was none other than The Great Beast himself, poured the contents of the golden bowl into the ink barrel. Incantations were muttered, weird hand gestures carved upon the gloomy air.

'The ink is ready, master,' muttered Crowley. He bowed deferentially before The Sage, though his own darker mind was already twisting over awful schemes.

'Then let the presses roll,' shrilled out Cefalu.

The trundling and clattering of the press began at last. The Sage hurried around to await the sheaths that would be fed off of the machine, eager to gaze upon the first printed pages of his life's work. As he hunched forward there, Mortimer Luminal, Crowley's second priest in their own offshoot of The Order, stepped up behind him. There was a barely perceptible nod from The Beast. Without a flicker of hesitation, Luminal drew a serrated dagger from beneath his robe, grabbed Cefalu by the hair, powerfully yanked his head back and sliced across the exposed throat. Cefalu barely had time to screech, his eyes flooding with terror and awful realisation. A shrill, joyous moaning wailed up from the acolytes at the delicious sight of spouting blood. Life pumping from his gaping throat, the mad-eyed Sage saw that all was over - that his death was fluttering down toward him like a hideous bat. He knew an instant eternity of despair - he would never come to read even a word of his completed masterpiece.

'The bowl,' barked Crowley. 'Let's not waste the stuff, my brethren. Bring the bowl. Look there on the first page. It is decreed and written by our Master himself...this book must have its blood...'

This book must have blood, and that is its Law...

These were the first sinister words, other than the gold-leafed title, that Faulkner read of the alleged original copy of *Diabolis Necrolatry*. He read as his wife and two children were upstairs sleeping. He was exhausted after a somewhat shocking day of 'work', but had told Cheryl that he had to rectify some glitch in the shop accounts - an excuse so that he could remain up a while and read a little of the fabled book that had so bizarrely worked its way into his possession. He snickered at the melodramatic tone of the opening sentences, but as the paragraphs unwound before his eyes, the superior sneer faded upon his face. His wife and children, sleeping so peacefully. Their warm, vulnerable throats flashed over and over in his mind. The serrated, black handled kitchen knife that he used as a letter opener was on the work top, easily within his reach. His knuckles whitened against the leather cover of the book, his slender hands trembling as he fought the urge to take up the knife.

The book had snaked its way to Faulkner in a complex, though perhaps inevitable, set of circumstances. A tragedy, or at least a gruesome death, had also come churning in its wake. He was a book dealer - mainly antiquarian, occult, pre-fifties first editions, ever-profitable rare erotica. He had a well run shop in Camden, an area with a high density of readers, and therefore of customers. Business had never been better. His life, all considered, was more than satisfactory. Though somewhat balder and slighter than he would have liked, he was doing well for himself and his family. Apart from that general sense of unease that troubles all intellectuals and those inclined to be 'bookish', he considered himself happy, successful, and damned good at his job. He traded, tracked down, acquired, swapped, bought and resold, and his day to day dealing with books and clients brought him great satisfaction. Naturally, in the course of his work, he had read the fable and lore surrounding the elusive limited first edition of the *Diabolis Necrolatry*. He was even in the process of writing an article on the thing himself - he regularly submitted to *The Antiquarian,* and was often published there, though at little fiscal profit. In the line of his work he had come across fading, crumpled second and third editions of the absurd book (the text of which was without grammar, punctuation, correct spelling and indeed few sentences of coherent, meaningful English) but of the six hundred and sixty-six that were said to have been printed on the private first run (Pendragon, Bloomsbury, 1919) he had not come upon so much as a fragment. The book had been written by a mentor and spiritual master of Aleister Crowley, that notorious drug addict and Black Magician of the early twentieth century. The ink used on that first run was alleged to contain the blood of new born infants, sacrificed in demonic rituals carried out purely for the purpose of infusing the book with the powers that the Black Sage had prophesised in his visions. The writer, Maximus Cefalu, vanished immediately after the printing of the Pendragon run, creating rumours that he had been murdered by the Satanic witches who ran the Pendragon house, and that his own blood had been mixed into the ink. The writer's cured skin and woven hair were used to bind and cover the first nine copies from the press. Of the original run, most had been burnt or destroyed by outraged Roman Catholic priests, who deemed the book an aberration against God, Art and Nature. A few copies were claimed to have been secreted out of the country to Europe by Crowley's sect. Whoever sets out to read the book, other than those initiated into the secrets of The Order Of The Golden Dawn, goes immediately insane. Or so it was said. The fact was that no single copy of the fabled first edition had ever been produced for examination, and the nonsense of the later editions is interpreted as an attempt by some writer or writers, as yet unknown, to parody rare occult writings and to ridicule the desire of those involved in antiquarian book circles to acquire such manuscripts.

Fully aware of this then, Faulkner had that morning been opening his business correspondence with his serrated kitchen knife, when a wild-haired vagrant came strutting into his shop, poisoning the air with his fox-rancid odour. He looked directly at Faulkner, his eyes shifty and malicious, then shuffled over to the Occult and Theology corner. There he hunched, paranoid, clawing over dust jackets, clucking quietly to himself, darting glances about the place. Faulkner decided to give him the benefit of the doubt (he had discovered that wandering types were often interested in theology and prepared to spend good, if dubiously acquired, money on the subject) and returned to his correspondence, mentally noting that he would give the fellow ten minutes browse-time before requesting him to leave. Five minutes later, when the shop had emptied but for the two of them, the derelict came striding up to the counter, fixing Faulkner with a manic stare.

'I have the book for you,' he yelped out. His Adam's-apple jerked up and down as he spoke, his throat skinny and grimy, like uncooked chicken skin. 'I have it! You want it!'

Faulkner, accustomed to eccentrics in his shop, retained his composure.

'I beg your pardon, sir?'

'The book....' The man's mad eyes darted to the door, around the corners, then back upon Faulkner.

'The *Necrolatry* of Cefalu,' he hissed. 'The cursed book.'

'Ah, *Diabolis Necrolatry*, I think you mean. I have it, sir. Two or three copies. I can get you one....'

'No, no, you young fool. To think is to mean, ha? Then is now, ha? I have it. I have one. You are interested.'

A statement, not a question. He prodded a yellow clawed finger toward Faulkner's chest.

'You, sir, are interested!'

The fellow was obviously a lunatic, and possibly dangerous. Faulkner knew he had to get rid of him as tactfully as possible. The last thing he wanted was an unsavoury incident in his shop.

'Like I say sir, I have two or three copies and I can't even sell those. Have you tried Jackson's down in the market?'

'Don't take me for a fool, boy. To see is to read!'

Faulkner flickered his superior, knowing smile. The best policy, he realised, was to simply diffuse the situation - calm the fellow, play along with him.

'Well, I suppose I'll have a browse over it. If it's a good copy, I might take it. What sort of condition did you say that it was in?'

The man's face quivered with rage.

'I have an original,' he fumed, 'in perfect condition. I'm fully aware that it's of great interest to you, Mister Faulkner. I've read your articles. I read everything ever written on it. All your work's there, in the appendix, for what it's worth. Even the item that you're working on now.'

Faulkner drew up to full height behind the counter, aware

that for once he perhaps had the physical advantage over the wastrel before him.

'Now sir, please don't take this the wrong way, but I must ask you to leave my shop. It's quite obvious that you're not well. I'm quite prepared to call the....'

The old man flapped his arms and waved Faulkner to silence.

'Oh, shush, and listen, you oaf! To think is to do. It's the real thing. I have one. Destined for you. Listen....'

He hauled himself straight in his festering raincoat. His eyes glazed over with the effort of memory, then he recounted, word for word, the very article that Faulkner was writing for *The Antiquarian*.

'*...I personally have only come across crumpled, fading second and third editions of the absurd book. The writing in these is without grammar, punctuation or correct English spelling - indeed, only a few sentences in the whole thing have any structure, coherence or meaning. Six hundred and sixty-six (yes, I'm afraid so!) copies were said to have been printed in the mythical first run (Pendragon, Bloomsbury, 1919) but I've yet to come upon so much as a fragment of one of these. The book was said to have been written by the spiritual master and mentor of the early twentieth century drug-fiend and Occult Magician, Aleister Crowley...*'

Faulkner reeled with the shock of this recital. The article, he knew, remained only on disc, incomplete, and emailed only yesterday as a first draft.

'*...Crowley, himself a writer of some merit, claimed that Cefalu placed several spells and evil curses upon the text. Such was the nature of this magic, that whenever the book was closed the actual words upon the pages would merge and reform, rearranging themselves in a logical and syntactical order that is not apparent in later editions of the book. The text had the power to alter its structure and meanings, blending them to the mould of the next reader's mind and subjective perceptions, thus each individual reader brought not just a new interpretation, but a whole new* *ordering to the writing...'*

Sentence after sentence, word for word, the article was recited. Faulkner leaned on his counter, rigid with the shock of the experience, yet with a sense of awakening and excitement. Here at last, after years of search and research, he stood on the threshold of a momentous, real life adventure. A mad man. A fabled book. The chance of discovery. He slowed a finger to his lips, silencing the old man, then strode across his shop to lock the door.

'I think I'll be closed a while,' he said. Despite his attempts to appear calm and in control of the situation, he was trembling from head to toe.

'Let me get this very clear,' he said, returning back behind his counter.

'You have an actual first edition of *Diabolis Necrolatry*?'

'I have.'

Faulkner hummed, fingering his letter opener.

'And somewhere within it are the words that you just recited - about the book itself?'

'In the ever changing appendix. Words by you. Or you yesterday. It's the nature of the thing. It's the book that...'

'Yes, yes,' cut in Faulkner. 'The book that writes itself. But my article isn't even published yet - it's only in draft form.'

This was met with a scorning sneer.

'The *Necrolatry* is not confined by time! It has no beginning but the reader. Its ending is in the final human mind. Mister Faulkner, you disappoint. It contains your work. Your scribbled contributions. At least it did so this morning. Much has been said and unsaid since then. But down to the heart of the matter. I know that you are looking for a copy. I read as much, which is why I looked you out.'

Faulkner, somewhat shaken from his solid ground, decided to call the bluff.

'It's an original edition?'

'I've said so. I may not look much, sir, but I'm an educated man of honour, and of my word. You don't think I look like this through choice, do you?'

He leaned forward over the counter, eyes pinning Faulkner's - eyes full of prowling and of pain. His rasping breath reeked of cabbage and sour wine.

'It's one of the first dozen or so. Bound in what I believe is Cefalu's own skin. Sometimes, when I read it, the thing slithers and contracts in my palms, heaves up from my fingers, as though it's trying to writhe away from me. It's like it's... it's like it's..'

Unable to find the words, he laughed. Dry, dusty laughter. Faulkner backed away from the breath-stench.

'I won't ask how you came by it.'

'Best not to know, Mister Faulkner. Not yet. Soon enough you'll read of my horrendous tale yourself, if you take it on. I'll sell you the thing, of course, and good riddance to it. But I'd advise you not to read from it. Not a word beyond the title. That's my advice, sir. I'm sure though, a man of your intelligence, when the time comes, you won't heed a word of it.'

'You make it sound like a challenge.'

'More like a curse.'

Faulkner laughed now. The situation was ridiculous. Absurd. A comical sketch. Yet here he was, being offered one of the most valuable first editions in occult literature, by a stinking mad man. All that mattered from here was that he confirm that it was a genuine copy, and settle a price. Of placing the book with a buyer - and at vast profit if he had the old fool marked properly - there would be no difficulty. He snapped into business mode.

'All right. Enough of this. How much?'

'Two thousand, sir. I'd ask more, personally. You know it's worth more. Much more. But the book instructed....'

'You'll want cash.'

'Naturally.'

'I'll have to inspect it. Maybe have it independently assessed.'

'I read as much this morning.'

'You have it with you?'

'No, no. It stays at home. You must come to my appartment tonight, at seven. Here's the address. You want Pimlico station, cross the main road, head for the bridge. Look out for the Morpeth Arms public house. I'm opposite. You'll find me.'

He handed Faulkner a scrap of paper, an address scrawled upon it.

'If I don't answer the door, just walk in. I'm often absorbed in my reading.' He sniggered as though he had made a good joke, displaying white gums and yellowed stumps of teeth. He stood there staring into Faulkner's face, awaiting the next move. There was something appalling in his glazed blue eyes; they did not focus on the foreground. Faulkner felt he was merely an incident of utter insignificance in a desolate landscape. The eyes were parallel, gaping upon infinity. Faulkner shivered, feeling total revulsion for the creature before him.

'Yes,' the old crone creaked out. 'The book brings great trouble to its reader. Thank God it's almost finished with me now. But heed me - take it on my word, and the look and the feel of the thing. Don't read it beyond the title. To a man such as yourself, its value is not in the text, but in the object itself. Sell it on. Take a holiday with your family on the profit. Mark me well sir, don't set out to read it.'

'Of course. It's the book that never ends....' Faulkner said in mockery, echoing one of the critical clichés about the book.

'It is indeed. But I've *almost* finished. Today I will. And then it's yours.'

'Two thousand.'

'Two thousand at seven.'

'I'll be there with cash.'

The old man gave a slow, single nod, swivelled away and seemed about to leave the shop. But, as if something had occurred to him, he turned back.

'Mister Faulkner, don't take all this too lightly.'

'I don't, sir. Neither the *Necrolatry*, nor you. Now if you'll excuse me, I'll reopen my shop.'

The old man jabbed his arm over the counter and grabbed up the letter opener. Faulkner stepped back, fearing the old loon was about to attack him, that other well-worn cliché about the book jarring into his mind.

'*This book must have its blood....*' The derelict said it for him, hissing out the very words.

'Would you care to do it now, Mister Faulkner, or would you prefer to keep the plot simple and do it later?'

'Do it? I don't know what you mean. Please, put that thing down. We've agreed a price and a time... please....'

The old lunatic swivelled the knife so that he held the blade between his fingers, offering it out to Faulkner as again his eyes glazed and he recited text from memory.

'*...Theo Faulkner stepped toward the pathetic old man, drawing the unsheathed knife from his coat pocket. It was a black handled, serrated kitchen knife that out of some habitual quirk he used as a letter opener for business correspondence. The old man stood there, eyes wide with terror, wild with the anticipation of pain. Faulkner strode forward, blade out, grabbing at the lapels of the man's jacket, brutally slashing across the pensioner's exposed white throat with the cruel blade....*'

He halted his recital, eyes narrowing onto Faulkner's.

'I read that this morning. The opening of the final chapter.

Now, or later, Mister Faulkner?'

Faulkner took the knife from his quivering hand and dropped it behind the counter. He knew that he could no more kill a stranger than he could his own children.

'Well...' he laughed cheerfully, attempting to defuse the situation with some humour, "Let's save the murder for later then... until after lunch at least!"

The old man shrugged, nodded politely, and was out of the shop door before Faulkner could recover enough composure to even ask his name.

The whole bizarre incident left Faulkner in a slight state of shock. He was distracted from the shop business for the rest of the day, and could concentrate on nothing but the idea of acquiring a first edition *Diabolis Necrolatry*. Barely able to await closing time, he took advantage of a lull and closed the shop early. He telephoned Cheryl to explain that he would be home late due to a business call, then made his way to a bank. He returned to the shop to lock and alarm up properly, and to collect the scrap of paper that held the old man's address. As he placed this in his wallet he thought over the whole incident. With time to consider the events, and in particular the fellow's awareness of his own recent writings on the *Necrolatry*, he was able to rationalise something of the inexplicable problem away. He had, after all, been writing his article on computer, and it probably existed on his hard-drive as a back up file as well as on disc. Any decent hacker would be able to access the file, and though the old man had not come across as computer literate, it was surprising how many unlikely people were indeed 'nerds'. Again, he had emailed a draft to *The Antiquarian*. It could well be that the old man had contacts there who had passed a copy of the file on to him, or even that he worked for the magazine himself. Faulkner's dealings with the publication had always been over cable. The fiend, for all he knew, could be the editor of the periodical, out-parodying him on his own spoof. Still, there had been something about the encounter that had been distinctly unsavoury and unwholesome. After placing the envelope of money securely in his inner breast pocket, he took up the letter-opener and placed it loose in the right hand pocket of his overcoat.

'Just in case,' he said aloud to the shop. He keyed in the alarm code and left the premises.

A tube journey later, Faulkner emerged into the white brightness of Pimlico. He had been there before of course, on visits to The Tate, but had forgotten how affluent and bohemian the area was. Certainly not the place you would expect a mad derelict to be residing. Taking directions from a newsagent, he followed the main road along to the bridge, and there took a left turn just before the river. Opposite the pub there was the house. A four storied, white fronted Edwardian terrace, it was far from the grubby ruin Faulkner had been expecting. The building was divided into flats, protected by security locks and intercoms. Even so, the street door was open. He rang the buzzer to the basement flat, read the surprising name there - Dr B Osburgh - and waited. No voice came over the intercom. He pressed again, then recalling the instructions, pushed the outer door open and walked into the hallway. A staircase led down on the right, and he hurried down, not wanting to encounter any other residents of the apartments. At the bottom there was only one door. He knocked politely, opened it, and calling out a cheery 'hello', entered the flat.

Music filtered from beyond the tiny hallway. He closed the door behind him. His nostrils twitched, the place stinking of vinegary sweat and decaying vegetables. The hallway led off into a kitchen. Faulkner shuddered away from all contact with the filthy surfaces and objects as he picked his way through. Chaotic mess littered the floor and every work top - half eaten, moulding meals on discarded plates, crumpled food packets, mould-filled cups and wine bottles, meat-flies lolling about the disgusting cooker and overflowing sink. It was the kitchen of an addict or a madman - a person too far removed from normal life to cook, eat or clean.

'Hello,' Faulkner called again, breathing in through his mouth to lessen the stench of the place.

'Doctor Osburgh? It's me. Theo Faulkner.'

A door was ajar at the far side of the kitchen, music lilting from within. Bolder now, Faulkner pushed through the door, then jolted with shock. The place was sparsely furnished, absent of all fuss or decoration. An ebony rocking chair with black leather cushions was the only seating, a small coffee table placed beside it, an open book resting on the table. In the room's far corner stood an archaic walnut cabinet with its built in radio, the control panel still glowing, music crisp and clear from the lower single speaker. Bookshelves lined the complete right hand wall, but these were bare, gaping empty, not a single book or ornament upon them. And there, dangling like a bizarre fruit in the centre of the room, hung the old stranger. A blue nylon washing line was tied to a hook in a ceiling beam and noosed tight around his neck, his face ghastly purple, eyes wide open. There was no movement. Once he had taken in the scene and steadied his nerves, Faulkner stepped across to the body, attempted to insert a finger between the cord and throat with the intention of loosening it, but his fingers were useless upon the hard nylon. Three weeks without food, three days without water, three minutes without air. He recalled the first-aid formula from a long-ago course, and though he was sure the old fellow had been hanging there for far longer than three minutes, his instinct was to attempt to save him. He looked around for scissors, or a knife - something to cut him down with so that he could loosen the noose. The letter opener, of course.

The old man dangled there, eyes wide and glazed with terror, wild in their suffering. Faulkner drew the unsheathed kitchen knife from his overcoat pocket and stepped forward. He grabbed the lapels of his jacket, stretched up, slashing the blade across the brutal cord.

Released, the body thumped to the bare floorboards of the room. Faulkner did a quick check. There was nothing - breathless, ice-cold and without pulse.

'How stupid,' he said as he crouched over the body. He had made a blunder getting this involved. It would have been better to have left him up there. When the police inevitably came upon the body, they would soon deduce that a second person had been upon the scene. No suicide ever cuts their own death-cord. There was no obvious note. Murder would be suspected. Perhaps he would find himself implicated. His name was even in the book. *The book!* It had to be the one squatting on the coffee table there, splayed open, cover upward. The cover appeared to be leather, the title and author in faded gold leaf lettering. He snatched it up, snapped it shut, and pocketed it along with the knife. He surveyed the room, the body. There was nothing more he could do here; nothing useful. Out of some misplaced sense of dignity and respect, he switched off the twittering radio, then he slipped away from the flat. Within a blur of minutes he was back down in the station, waiting for his connection home. The money was still in its envelope, but it was the book that was burning in his pocket. He dare not take it and read from it here. Nor even on the tube ride home. Instead he stared at the advertisement posters, his mind in utter confusion.

Theo Faulkner. Bespectacled, balding, but possessing a keen intelligence. Married with two children, a lovely home, a flourishing and enjoyable business. He was reasonably happy with his life. There was nothing that he wanted to jeopardise with recklessness, even if he did consider himself something of an adventurer; an explorer in the dark-lands of the human mind. But that night he took out the *Diabolis Necrolatry*. He fingered the dry leather cover. Around him the house was in silence. Outside it was dark, the street beyond his study window deserted. Could it really be that this was human skin that he fingered? The grain was fine, the texture cool and smooth. As he let his fingers wander over the gold lettering his stomach crawled with butterflies. Years of hearsay and fumbling, frustrated research, and now here was the real thing before him. How could he possibly resist, despite the old doctor's warning and a wealth of cautionary lore? He allowed the book to fall open toward its centre. At last, in this, he was doing something tangibly brave. The very reading of the *Necrolatry*, decoding the damned and cursed text, would be his *heroic* deed. He listened attentively. Not so much as a murmur from upstairs. Cheryl had gone to bed a good hour before, leaving him to 'work on the books.' The children had been asleep long before that. He could read at his leisure now, until tiredness overcame him, and there would be no disturbance or intrusion. His eyes fell to the top of the right hand page. The ink was purplish black, the print tiny. The words seemed to swim and buckle before his eyes, floating and moving upon the yellowed page, relocating and reordering themselves. When he did manage to settle his eyes and read a complete sentence, he sniggered aloud at the absurd, inevitable line:

'*This book must have blood, and that is its Law ...*'

He blinked hard, screwed his eyes shut a few seconds to

settle them, then read on. His courage faltered as he skimmed past that opening line. Words swam up toward him from the page, physically worming their way through the space between his eyes and the paper. Beneath the swirling soup of those words he could see figures and scenes, as if the actual page were a screen, a magical scrine, visions within smoking up, presenting themselves to his imagination. The Black Sage hunched in the dim corner of a brick walled basement, ancient presses set up for a print run in the gas-light of the shadowed room. Young men in work smocks were crouched on the floor, working over printing blocks, setting them up for the press. Next he saw himself in the doorway of his own shop, fumbling with keys, the shelves within emptied, barren, his business somehow finished and ruined.

This book must have its blood, so it is said. Theodore Faulkner, withered, balding, bespectacled, ramshackle. He locked up his derelict shop for the final time. His withering business had been sold on to support the habits of vice and addiction that had overtaken his life since the cruel and brutal murders of his wife and children - could it really have only been three years ago? Just three years. Back then he had enjoyed a lovely home, a devoted wife, two lovely children. His business had been flourishing, and he was reasonably happy with his lot...

Faulkner watched himself upon the page, taking up a knife, walking up the staircase of his own home. He tried to stop reading, to avert his eyes. His knuckles whitened against the black leather of the cover. The book seemed to throb and twitch within his fingers, as though it were indeed a living creature. In tearing his eyes from the page his gaze fell upon the kitchen knife. Despite his will, his eyes swivelled back over the page. There, beneath the words, flashed visions of white, vulnerable throats. Heads yanked back. The knife was in his hands. The faces were of his own children and his wife, deep and serene in sleep. Their throats exposed. His pale, narrow hands began to tremble. He would have dashed the unholy object to the study floor but because of the nature of the curse he could not.

'*This book must have blood, and that is its Law, but who would have thought that this contented, rational man could prove such a demonic fiend as to butcher in cold blood his own...*'

Faulkner's eyes jarred up as he tried to avoid the emerging words. The knife was in his hand. He approached the doorway and stepped out onto the staircase of his own home. He tried to avoid the floating words, the book throbbing and writhing within his grasp like a warm serpent.

'*...such brutal barbarity that he would later cover by...a convenient and silent alibi...no evidence linking him to either crime....*'

The words wormed up, offering him an escape. Smiling now, possessed by demonical lust, the knife was in one hand, the thirsty book in the other. He could barely wait to see the warm blood spilling over the sheets and pillowcases. Faulkner tried to avert his eyes. He tried to drag his enslaved mind away from the text. But he could not stop himself from reading. He could not stop himself completing the horrendous page....

Everybody Got a Jane

Neil Benbow

So here's mine. Tall, thin, blonde and beautiful. Fucked up in that special way only beautiful women are when they come from a spoiling love which they felt as poverty. Fucked up by regard given for good looks rather than personality. Fucked up by attention given for all the wrong reasons, or so they will tell you. Fucked up by the prizes that follow from all of these and hollowness that needs to be filled by something, anything, and anyone, any obsession for now. Everybody got a Jane. It's a rite of passage to be gone through. Some make it out sane, some not. Some die late, embittered, burnt fingers chafing into the long nights that follow. When we first met I never noticed her, not in any ignorant way, but more of a 'there's this great looking woman over there, I'm here, she's with someone else, that's it.' Then we spoiled it. But wait.

We worked together and I never realised that she was falling in love with me. Or so she told later. One day, cycling, my pride and joy new mountain bike, bicycle shorts all Lycra and Chamois. She smiled lips open and wide, wanting to be going with me. Then later, she came around with a card and a present for my birthday, spreading her blue cotton dress across the floor, wishing me well and, well, she cried. Over what I didn't know but I wanted her to stop crying, and to do other things that before had never entered my mind about her. Thinking, just what was this about? This present then tears thing?

But this is too quick. Months passed between my first meeting, working with her and this. But then that's how we were, we moved pretty quick. We went out for beer, just a drink to show her around. Her man, never mentioned, never asked after. She drank easy, pouring and ordering relaxed and slow with smiles for barmen and barmaids, glasses ready to be filled, just for that smile from her again. We talked of life, music - my passion, drama - hers, and anything else that helped touch the sides. I was only too happy to be with this beautiful creature who laughed at everything I said and smiled at life. Later I took her back to my rooms, she sipping vodka bought on the way. On the edge of my unmade bed, she cold and wet from the rain. Taking her clothes off to keep warm in my old sweatshirt and teeth chattering, what else could I do but want to warm her? Her tales of unlove in a coldened marriage, what else but to hold and want her better? Then the touching, holding, fingers here and there, kisses and calls in the air between us. Fumbles and fingers caressing, losing mind, gaining feelings, rushes and blushes. Feeling her warmth and wet, entering, gaining momentum only to be thrown out by her body, pushed out and wanting in, hushed voice telling of wrongness but wanting, whispers of please, but please don't, then hands finding and encouraging. Falling asleep to wake cold and alone, a note of having to raise children from beds, attend to toast and schools.

Thinking of what had happened and whys of the evening before.

To meet again later at work, nothing said or hinted, smiles exchanged, over break, we must talk, meet later. Timings arranged, other events changed to make space. Her arriving later with vodka and smiles, a newer white, crisp cotton dress, outlines suggesting stockings and sex to come. Me listening of love but no promises of futures as the vodka passed between us. Listening to words but wanting else. Listening, watching lips, blue eyes in concentration while time passed, then hands reaching, pulling toward, breasts offered and taken.

Some habits take aeons to accrue, others happen despite awareness. We settled soon into patterns of she arriving after kid bedtimes, vodka in hand and tales of woe, needing to stare into space while chewing on inner cheek. I would read, watch TV. Until that too would distract. Her need for me was to be her space, still, existing in non-existence until her meditation on inner demons was done. I was Sir Galahad, all knights rolled into one, and I could do this until her dragons were set in stone.

Then we would make love, slow, gentle easing into the night. Inventive, touchy feely stuff you read about in books, where each time passion increases as tempo slows. Me incredulous that she could be so turned on by me, her wetness flowing to soak sheets and me.

Many times I awoke, hands clutching into blanket, holding on to not knowing what. Darkness everywhere and hearing her breathing, deep and low, body angled into dreams. Knowing later but never wanting to ever know, that love created in this way - spoiled, rotten and wrong - creates the best sex: intense, passionate and of course, doomed. A love doomed to build death, hate and poison that would take years to wash away.

The vodka would give permission to speak; she talked of frustrations and lovers who missed her by their needs. I heard the warnings but wanted anyway. She talked of foods and not needing to eat, the need to be slim, retain her shape: after two kids it was pretty good eh? All was information to me, where this, we were going never entered my head. We had our space in my rooms, tight under the eaves, safe from the world, who could need more?

We went to Spain, travelling across France, staying in cheap dingy rooms that she couldn't afford but complained bitterly of. To Pamplona, me for the first time noticing how the vodka level slipped down the bottle, how food necessary for me was wasted for her. Her drunk in the afternoon, sliding through streets, hanging off my arm, pulling me down, asleep on a bench beside some fountain in the park, snoring, bag rattled across the ground strewn cosmetics, passport and toothbrush. The last not making sense until much later.

Yet. Siesta's cooler evenings stretched on cotton sheets in hotels, she sucking me until I would beg for release, as good as love ever gets. To lie together as ceiling fans spin flies into oblivion.

Baguettes better thrown in temper rather than eaten. Anger at my raising at her lack of food. Distractions of rough foreplay, her need to be spanked, I dumb as only young in love men can be. Loving in place of fighting, or was it the other way round?

My inarticulacy stares at me across the page. I loved with all that I had, and yet did not have enough. I could not make her happy but thought, like some school report come to haunt, I could try harder. Chasing my tail and hers across a continent, complete in misery, as she wanted more, more that she was not able to verbalise otherwise the need transmuted and lost. A guessing game with only losers as the prize. Watching her flirt with strangers and then being needed to pick up the pieces when such went astray. Hearing her moans of bottom pinchers but catching her glances to entice. My jealousy spurred her further, yet I did not know how to let go. Despising myself for knowing my weaknesses and still being around or wanting more, masochism or abuse? How close together these were. I would break free for a few days until she would return bearing gifts to beat on my door, seeking forgiveness or needing solace supposedly only I could offer. I could not refuse her though I tried other lovers; they and their own peculiarities would seem pale. We would make love instantly to stave recriminations, questions, though these would arrive dressed in rags in later conversation.

As our time moved on she felt need to be in company though quickly despised all friends and acquaintances, rubbished overtures from all. Her drinking now not easy but forced and gulped, time running out. Nagging that I could not fulfil her. Snarls at words not wanted or wanted heard. Here visits grew infrequent and missing her became painful but welcome, then she would return, all smiles, love and gifts of welcome. I wondered at the guilt of her gifts. Friends told of sightings drunk at parties; I nodded my hearing, pondering of their inability to see my pain. Then a party together, late, missing her presence, finding her in the arms of a stranger, his hands on her white knickers, her kissing him not seeing me, the light shaded but strong enough to burn holes that last forever. I left, she coming after me, apologies, blaming drink, the moment, and a forceful other. Me cold and angry, into the pit all cuckolds hide to escape the gaze of others' knowing glances. We fought for the first time. Wanting to hit her, using words as fists, her scraping, scratching, and despising my weakness for her deeply as I did. The morning bleak, eyes weary with sight, running away determined to never answer her calls.

Of course she came back, vodka in hand, now wanting to smoke dope to ease the drinking. Wanting to try eating, wanting meals bought only in good restaurants. My now seeing her rise immediately after eating to take her bag, go the toilet and return with freshly brushed teeth. Resentment rising in me as I paid good food bills for her to vomit them away. My weariness at the binges that sapped me but somehow strengthened her. Feeling the failure that comes from wanting the best for another, wanting to help but slipping surely into control, into helping when leaving would be better.

One summer week, she nightly picking me up from work, buying vodka for us and pizza for me. Drinking, me watching videos while she reflected, sparking cigarettes off the stove, taking me to work, to follow the ritual again. Then, finding myself walking the road for extra vodka, catching myself and recognising that this was out of control: 7 bottles in 6 days. Too drunk to run away or change the day but still knowing that this could not continue.

More fights, arguments, other lovers, a litany of shame that in its making saps and contorts to destroy better being. My understanding over and over the pull of moth from bright candle flame, the suck of fingers into fire. I was in deteriorating orbit, pulled closer by another's gravity, shamed by debauch. I continued to leave. To leave. To return. The gaps of days became weeks; slowly immeasurably her influence waned. Then. A call, again late night, needing me immediately, getting out of bed, dressed to attend. She phoned again, apologies, emergency over. Feeling stupid at being caught by her until she asked to see me in the morning 'sober' to 'talk.'

I arrived, no answer to my knock on the door, checking my time, trying the back door finding it open, calling for answer. I climbed the stairs fearful of what I might find. She asleep.

Alone. Relieved but concerned over what emergency had taken place here. She stirring, eyes baggy in the sunlight, breasts droopy in dressing gown, looking for cigarettes. Asking what I was doing there, no memory of phone calls. I made her coffee as she bathed, not wanting to notice the beer cans, different brand cigarette packs or the empty condom pack. Wanting to leave. This was no longer of my concern; I was trying to leave her, not be caught again. Drinking coffee, Jane now dressed and made up for the day, me wanting to be anywhere but here. With foresight I'd made plans to meet a friend later. She wanting to go out, talk, be friends, my senses taut as in the presence of any predator. I left after agreeing to meet that night, though I felt the yellow streak on my back pressing deeper into flesh and psyche.

We met for drinks of course; she was burning slow, angry, biting into me, until finally I said I would leave. Outside, the night dark and cloudy as she began telling me of my uselessness, my inadequacies, how she'd heard I was seeing another. Then she attacked, nails in my face, hands pulling my hair, me twisting as she grabbed for my balls, falling to the floor, hearing others laugh at the spectacle as she tried to kick. I waited, knowing that this would end. Cold, lying on the ground feeling the pain but feeling release in an inner complete and contented way. I knew now that I would never return, could never return. I had finally been ravaged and needed no more. She laughed as I struggled to my feet and said my goodbyes, believing that I would return. I always had before...

That would be a nice end, eh? And it did feel like one, though life being savage as it is and we would/will but deny it: a month later, a dark late night of rain and swift winds, I lay in bed watching tv and heard a knock at the door. It was Jane. Drunk and inflamed, all made up with perhaps nowhere to go, holding onto the door and wanting to talk. I allowed her in.

She needed coffee she said and, making it, I heard the storm approaching. She questioned of newer loves and places I'd been, of missing her and stories she'd heard from others of her kicking me to the floor. She threw her coffee at me, kicked, missed, and kicked again. Asking her to leave passioned her further, she ran to my room throwing records, music, hi fi to the floor. Then she fell onto the bed, begging to stay, asking for love, forgiveness. Then she fell asleep. I picked up my papers and music and began tidying as she slightly snored. I wanted her gone, picking her up roused her, I threatened a bath to sober her, she screamed at me to let her go, she began kicking blindly at me again and I pinioned her. I would not have taken these things from a man; she knew these things yet still demanded special privilege. I carried her to the door, she screaming, biting, gouging at my balls. Finally I pushed her through the door, she screamed that I would pay for this and was gone.

The police arrived hours later, just when I thought it all over, accusing me of battery, assault and actual bodily harm. I went with them, but making sure that others who had been in the house made their statements too. Jane hawked photographs of bruises telling tales of violence to all who might listen. My embarrassment somewhere turned to shame at being involved in this: denial was pointless as was the showing of my bruises, cuts and hurt. Janes win in the short term by their lack of shame and who cares for the long term these days? Nobody of that time matters to me now except in the few times of self-reflection such as these. The police saw the situation as it was, suggested that I never let her in again, to ignore her, no matter what. All good advice only perhaps now for the first time I heard the truth in it, but isn't that how advice is? Only useful at the right time or when we're ready to hear it...

She called many times afterwards, always late, drunk of

course, mumbling incoherently, as I continued to ignore her pleas. She continued rubbishing me with others. Once I saw her walking toward me, and I ducked away, not needing any further reminders.

I believe at the time I loved her, though I know I will not ever love again in such a way. I learned and that's all any of us can ever hope to gain from any relationship. Learning the features of such relationships, obsessive, co-dependent, fucked up, call it what you will: the sex being the best ever, the over concern for another, the wanting to make them happy, the continuing despite shame, loss of friends, self respect and on...

Everybody got a Jane: I'm over mine now. Aren't I?

The Man Who Left Himself

John Barfoot

Things narrowed down when she left you, that's when the walking started. Three months and you haven't stopped yet.

Pine-smell, insect-hum, green light. Outside things. Things you can walk away from. Repetition, that's all that's needed. One foot in front of the other. Automatic. No thought required. Just keep walking.

You walk and you're wishing again that you could walk out of your mind, when the path turns suddenly. The trees fall away and you're blinded by sunshine. You blink, shade your eyes and when your vision comes back, there's a big house ahead. It's not so much the fact of the house itself that's unexpected, more its style. Bay-windowed, slate-roofed, iron-railinged. A Victorian three-storey, alone at the foot of the mountain, so incongruous that your sense of scale wavers. It makes the mountain look small.

You look at the map. Nothing. Not even an indication of ruins. But then you're not even sure where you are. The recommended approach route wasn't where the book of walks said it should be. The tangle of lanes and farm tracks spun you round and threw you out at a car park. Not Forestry Commission - no tattered Watch Out, There's A Thief About! poster - but cars already standing, even this early in the morning, and beyond them, a half-hidden yellow arrow, pointing into the trees.

It wasn't until you walked past the first one and noticed the layer of pine needles on roof and bonnet, the chrome spotted with brown rust, that you realised the cars were abandoned. Six of them, neatly parked. No external damage, but when you peered inside you saw steering wheels fat with mould, driving shoes curled up like caterpillars, road atlases like soft paper explosions. None of your business. That's what you thought, wasn't it? Head too full already. But the hulks you saw further on into the trees, the lines of cars silted into small brown hills, they made you pause to wonder. There must have been some reason to come here at one time. All these cars. Who left them?

When did the forest start moving back in? Perhaps the attraction disappeared, people started using the site to dump old vehicles. That would have been some time ago, judging by the outmoded lines of some of the more recognisable carcasses. How else explain all this decayed metal? Why bother explain? Your business is to walk. What you walk through is incidental.

The house. Maybe that's what they came for. The house the map says doesn't exist. So what? It's there, in front of you. Smoke rising from a stack of chimneys. Flowers nodding gently in the garden at the front. The tiny rock pool with its murmuring fountain and fishing gnome. A small bird perched on the wooden board tied to the railings. Sandwiches, Pastries, Drinks. Well-executed Italic lettering. A professional job. You shoved something to eat in your rucksack earlier this morning, spooned some coffee powder into a flask of hot water. You don't need anything. But you're curious. Who lives here in such spectacular isolation? The big front door is open. You push the black-painted iron gate aside and walk up the path.

Inside, a wooden hand leaning against the bottom step of the staircase points to the left. The light's dim, the stair-landing gloomy and indistinct. You have an impression of a group of small figures, pale, the size of six-year olds, pressed together behind railings at the top. They're like big after-images on your eyeballs. You decide that's what they are, because when you move your eyes, some of them seem to move with you. They cluster on the walls and ceiling, then dim and fade into designs on the old, ornate wallpaper.

You're conscious suddenly that there may be someone in the shadows up there and for a moment it's you all those weeks ago: invisible, watching her leave. She stood at the door the way you're standing now, looked up at you in silence. She couldn't see you but she knew you were there. She stayed that way until someone called her name, softly, from outside. From the top of the stairs you watched the door close behind her. She took care to do it quietly.

If someone's there now - invisible, watching - you don't want to stare at them. You drop your head and go into the room indicated by the hand.

Sunshine falls through a big bay window onto a white chill cabinet. Its shelves are stacked high with sandwiches and cakes of all descriptions, as if a rush is expected. An old lady with grey hair coiled and pinned into a bun is perched on a high-legged stool behind a tiled counter. She's big, bloated, soft-looking wearing the sort of old-fashioned housecoat your grandmother wore when she went fat. She's already looking at you when you come through the door.

You drop your eyes and say, reluctantly, 'Good morning.'

When you look back up she's still staring at you. Her eyes are searching your face. It's as if she half recognises you, but wants to be sure. Whatever she's looking for, she seems to find it. She grunts, not unpleasantly, and turns to the view behind her. An upward-sloping green field dotted with enormous house-sized rocks. Dark mountain slopes, like the gathered skirts of a giant lady. A fringe of trees across the peak.

You turn to the cabinet. Neatly printed paper flags stuck into each sandwich identify chicken, brie, cranberry, bacon, ham, smoked salmon, houmous, olives, coleslaw; much more. A framed card on the counter lists ciabatta, foccaccia, pitta, nan, pumpernickel, soda-bread, nut-bread. It's very tempting. You realise you feel hungry. It's not something you've bothered with lately. But the dry tuna in the cling-filmed rolls in your rucksack seems dull suddenly. You look over what's on offer, get lost for a while in the little chilled world before you, settling eventually on a huge foccaccia salad concoction and reach in to get it.

The old lady is still looking out at the view. There's something odd about her contemplation of it. Not as if she's enthralled by the beauties of landscape. More on the lookout for something. Daren't look away for too long. Might miss it. You cough and shuffle. Her head doesn't move. You tap a coin gently on the glass front of the cabinet. Nothing.

'Can I buy this sandwich, please?'

It comes out louder and ruder than you intended, and she turns quickly, as if hearing intruders. She looks over your head at the door. Then her gaze lowers by degrees until, at last, you are in it. Your face is half-apologetic but surly as well, as if you won't be put upon. She stares at you for a few moments, then extends a large woven-raffia paddle. You start to put coins on it. She shakes her head, nods at the sandwich. You put it on the paddle and she whisks it away, holds it up close to her face, turns it until the little adhesive label on the cellophane wrapper is directly in front of her eyes.

'Pound,' she says quietly.

You hear her voice as water trickling in a dried-up stream, making water-noises for the last time before sinking into baked mud.

She swings the paddle back and waits, not looking directly at you, patient. You didn't see the label. A pound is amazing for any sandwich these days, but certainly for this one. You select one coin from those in your hand, take the sandwich, and put the coin on the paddle. She smiles at you briefly, then tips the money into a box behind the counter. She turns back to the window, settles herself on the stool with a sound like quills rattling and stilling. She has not been unkind but you feel as if you have ceased to exist. There is a certain comfort in this.

For a moment, while the house ticks quietly in the sunshine and dust motes shower down around your head, you consider continuing to stand there. Ignored.

The moment passes.

'Goodbye.'

Your word sinks into the same baked mud as her voice. She doesn't look round, just lifts the fan and lets it fall. She could be acknowledging you or merely adjusting her position. What she is interested in is out there, in the landscape the window frames like a cinema screen.

Before stepping out of the front door into the sunshine, you glance up the stairs. Your eyes have adjusted. This time the darkness is complete. But odd sounds are coming from the gloom at the end of the landing. Faint, delicate rustling that makes you think of dry leaves on a parquet floor. Quietly exuberant whoops and squeaks, voice-like, as if someone's spinning the tuning knob of an old-fashioned radio. The sounds stop as you listen, as if a door has been closed on children, and, for a moment, you think something huge and pale is looking at you through the banister rails. It's gone almost before it registers, but you're left with a feeling of some benign but distant curiosity.

You're doing it again. Staring. You remember that time you looked up from your book and she was staring at you. You said, 'What?' and she said, 'Nothing.' You said, 'No, what?' and she just turned away.

Since then you've had this feeling that something creeps out of you when you're absorbed, when your guard's down. She saw it. Now that she's gone it's free to come out at any time. You're waiting for it. When you see it, you'll understand. That's what you think.

You drop your head and hurry out into the light.

The footpath begins to climb immediately beyond the house. It's clearly visible far ahead, zig-zagging up the flank of the mountain. You stop to put the sandwich away in your rucksack, then start up at a brisk pace. You don't allow yourself to slow as the slope increases; you never do. A steady, undemanding climb, that's what it looked like from below. Now it's turned into a steep, precipitous ascent. Your legs are burning. Blood's rushing and thumping in your ears. You're starting to pant like some primitive engine. It has become important to maintain the pressure each day. You're used to the feeling by now. No mercy, no quarter.

But you can't keep it up indefinitely. You have to stop, throw off your pack, fall to your hands and knees on a little flat grassy place at the side of the path. Your chest is heaving. Black spots dance in red mist behind your eyes. Your hair feels wet. Your glasses are steamed up. Sweat's running down your back. You stay like that, kneeling, for some time. Slowing down. Panting yourself back to life. Feeling dry grass rough on the palms of your hands. Cool air playing on the back of your neck.

You raise your head and look out from your vantage point. You're much higher than you realised. There's a sort of baked silence up here, and the old house looks tiny. It's like a miniature building set down in the compressed landscape of a model railway layout. Pale blobs, lots of them, are moving slowly in random patterns in a large garden at the back. Children? The scale seems wrong, somehow. They're too big, their movements too abrupt and jerky. And yet your overall impression is of some child-like game, obscure but meaningful.

You promise yourself you'll try to join in if they're still there on your way back to the car. Lean on the wall and watch for a while. Then walk over and say something. It sounds easy. You're not worrying about what to say or how to say it.

You rummage around in the rucksack for your binoculars. You'd like to take a closer look. The sandwich comes to hand first. At once, you realise you're hungry. You make yourself comfortable. Tear the cellophane wrapper off with your teeth.

Start to eat. The first bite confirms that this is a superior sandwich. Ridiculously good value for a pound. Chewy foccaccia crust with a faint fried taste to it. Soft white bread underneath. Fresh crisp tomato. Crunchy Chinese leaf. Cucumber, red cabbage, pitted olives. Other tastes not immediately identifiable. The tomato in particular is excellent. You're not normally much of a tomato man, regard it mainly as a garnish for other things more interesting. But this is marvellous. Soft but not pulpy flesh, and lots of seeds in almost a syrupy liquid at the centre of each slice. The seeds are unexpectedly delicious. Their own taste is so faint as to be almost indistinguishable, but they lend a texture and a tang to the other ingredients. It is, you find yourself thinking with some surprise, heavenly.

You've worked your way round the edges of the huge concoction, now you bite into the centre. To your disgust, your teeth grate on something solid. They break through some sort of shell, meet in a soft but gritty substance. Whatever it is, it moves. Wriggles frantically in your mouth. There are legs, lots of them. You choke, spit the whole mouthful out onto the grass. Hawk. Cough. Again and again, until nothing is left.

The thing is a good two inches long. Lying like a flattened white gherkin in the wreckage of your ejected mouthful. Short black legs flutter feebly all along its length, like oars on a rammed galley. Green stuff oozes sluggishly from the place where you almost bit it in two. A steady stream of thick white liquid pulses glutinously from the tail.

You stare in horror. Two stubby antennae wave feebly as you bend closer to see what you almost swallowed. The gorge rises in your throat. The white liquid looks thick and glutinous because it is full of eggs. The tomato seeds you have been eating and relishing - they're insect eggs.

You're violently sick. Nose as well as mouth. The jet is so

strong it splashes on the rocks at the side of the path and spatters your bare legs. Heave after heave trying to turn you inside out. Making your stomach ache as if someone's punched you.

When your eyes clear, you stare at the mess. Grass blades poke up through it here and there. Eggs are quite clearly discernible. They're already bigger than those still squirting from the mother. Little wriggling forms can be seen through the jelly-like exteriors.

Something moves suddenly in your stomach. You've never felt that before. Independent movement inside you. It moves again convulsively. Stills. More stirring, in a different place this time. Sluggish, then lively.

You hold your breath, try to kill thought, as if you're trying to escape the attentions of something outside your body. Something that will go away if you can erase yourself from its senses.

More movement. Frantic this time. Crawling. Climbing. They're waking up. Growing already. Scrabbling and scuttling in the bag of your stomach. Stillness comes again, but it's tense, knotted with expectation. Your body goes cold as ice. You feel your scrotum draw up tight, every hair stand erect.

Frenzied churning begins, all at once, and the first pain comes. It's a burrowing pain. They're biting. Eating. Invading the meat you're made of. They're inside you and they're trying to get out.

You pull your T-shirt off and throw it aside. Waves tremble across your belly. It's all happening very fast. You're screaming and you know you're going to die. You've known for so long it's like you remember. Inside you. It's always been inside you. You've carried it with you all your life. She saw it. She saw it and left you. Insects are rioting in your brain like fireworks, sparking momentary images, smells, memories. It could have made sense. Easily. She might have stayed. You can see that now, how it could have been true. Now it's too late.

Insects boil out of your body in a white froth and all at once, so suddenly that the past ceases to exist, your body's discarded. It falls and dwindles. You're released. You're free.

One of your stragglers plops fatly to the ground, struggles in a tiny cage of dried grass, frees itself and scampers away, over pebbles and dirt, to join the others. You're gathered along the edge of the path leading down to the house.

There is a place for you after all. Someone's sitting in the big bay window. She's been watching out, waiting for you to come. And suddenly you're in motion. Tumbling, falling, swarming down the mountain.

She sees you now. You're flowing over rocks and grass like a white tide.

She has stilled her woven-raffia fan. She has caught her breath.

She is leaning forward.

English Electric

Simon Crump

I shut my eyes and it starts. A mucky pink dress, scabby knees and scuffed red sandals. I hear screaming and taste smoke. I open my eyes then close them again. It's quiet. The flesh is bubbling black.

I get off the bed, go downstairs and stick the kettle on. I take my mug through to the shed. It's getting light and I've got to make a start. I get my tools, the list, and my bag of metal plates. I reckon there's three to do today, but I take them all just in case. Since she left it's public transport or shankses for me. It's going to take a while.

*

This old street's had it. Worn away, slowed down, furred up and knackered. All my life it's been fading out and today it's finally broken. Seized. Locked-up solid. Most of the shops are boarded-up, burnt-out or both. The only ones doing business are Everything's A Pound. There's still the little baker's on the corner. It's been there since I was a kid. I go in to get a sarnie, so I can smoke without feeling sick. The lady who runs it is two days older than water. Her hands are shaking so badly she can hardly get her fingers in the till. Under the glass-topped counter there's a faded card specked with fly shit. Trembly letters read CAKES FOR THE SPECIAL OCCASION. Next to it on a paper plate there's an example of the old girl's handiwork. It's the wrong colour for food, more grey than brown. Halfway down the filling's oozing out like pus from a bedsore. White blackmail note caps scrawled across the top say LIFE BENIGS AT FORTY and she's crammed a stockade of 40 candles round the edge. Most of them have been lit before and the cake slumps way off to the right. It looks like a scale model of a mining disaster.

I have to cut through town for the first one. Every second person looks insane. The man ahead of me in the post office queue bursts into song, then into tears. Outside in the street there's a young couple screaming at each other. Two feet away their son sits roaring in a knackered pushchair, great wicks of snot oozing down his face.

The bus pulls into the station - the Transport Interchange - and I get on. I sit right at the back, as far away from the driver as possible. I'm the only passenger. It swings out of the Interchange, up the hill out of town and threads its way past 80s' Tory visions of home ownership for all. Lace curtains bunched up like saucy underwear hang at newly installed diamond-leaded UPVC windows. Porcelain figurines, painted by internationally renowned porcelain figurine painters, gaze out onto shiny Ford Fiestas parked on freshly block-paved driveways. Outposts of neat gentility. Tiny islands of respectability, cut off then paralysed by the swamp, the biggest, bleakest most brain-rottingly depressing council estate in Europe.

I get off the bus in the dead centre of the estate. The air tastes of polythene and somebody's smashed a toilet on the footpath. I pick my way through china-studded dogshit and I see two kids crouching in some bushes doing god knows what with carriers and an aerosol. First on the list today is at the tail-end of a cul-de-sac about five minutes walk away.

Chadwick Road Substation No 549

A baby this one and amongst my favourites. Built in the 1930s, massively over-engineered and still going strong, last link in the chain from power station to domestic fuse box.

All the equipment exposed, not bricked up anyway, protected from the elements by curved Morris Minor-style sheet-metal cabinets, painted green and padlocked. A bank of forward-winch Reyrolle circuit breakers connect a flat copper busbar supplying 11 thousand volts to a pair of humming oil-cooled transformers which step the power down to 415 volts.

Inside a heavy cast-iron cupboard a Low Voltage Board carries an array of 400 amp fuses with brass contacts, each one capped with a knobbly white porcelain grip the size of a Cornish pasty. At the base of the cabinet the outgoing cables are tapped through 30 amp cartridge fuse boxes to a timer which controls the street lamps. Then the cables wriggle down into a pit and slither out under the streets. Next stop is your house.

Back at the bus stop there's a man waiting. Camouflage gear, a swallow on his neck and a blotched purple face. The kind of face that's been in lots of pubs and too many fights. He starts rolling a fag. I unzip my bag, rummage for my baccy tin and begin rolling one myself, first smoke of the day.

Out the corner of my eye I see him spark up and I wonder if he's thinking what I'm thinking. He takes the first drag.

The bus turns up, right on cue. He chucks the fag in the road, gobs, then turns and cracks me a grin,

'Never fucking fails, does it pal?'

*

I was doing alright. I'd worked hard at school. I stayed in most nights studying while my mates were out getting pissed on Strongbow and trying to shag some lass or other. I read books without being told. Used words that got the piss taken out of me. I got decent O levels and went straight into an apprenticeship at Tyzacks.

Tyzacks manufactured tools, everything from sets of screwdrivers right up to agricultural tools - hydraulic fitments for tractors, machine sections for bailers, chaff-cutting knives for combines and threshing machines. They set me on a lathe in machine shop No 7 where they made the really big stuff.

By the time they'd taught me to use it, I could scan a blueprint, read off the specs and turn a chunk of steel into something useful. I got to use my brain and my hands. I loved it. I did day release at tech for two years and passed City & Guilds Workshop Practice first time. Five years later Tyzacks made me foreman. Youngest ever in the history of the firm. I got my photo in the paper.

Day to day, my job as foreman meant wandering about with a clipboard, drinking far too much tea and ordering in the right materials to get the stuff made. I missed working with my hands, the satisfaction of making something, but at least I was still with the lads on the shop floor and the money was better.

Twice a week I'd take my order dockets up to accounts to have them processed - which is where I met Nichola.

I only asked her out for a bet. She was one of those lasses who acted like they were special, just that little bit better than everybody else, and I didn't think she'd look twice at me. First date we ever had it turned out she had a sense of humour. She let me kiss her.

We married three years later and six months after that Nichola got her job at Abbey National. In those days Abbey gave cheap mortgages to all their staff. We moved out of our little rented place into a house of our own; just around the corner from my folks, decent shops close by, a good-sized spare room and a tiny garden just big enough for a swing

I'd go for a pint after work sometimes and talk shit with the lads from Tyzacks. Nichola went out with her mates from Abbey, talked about the Royal Family, babies, periods or whatever it is women talk about when they get together, and on Saturday mornings we'd both hit B&Q. We'd spend the rest of the weekend Doing It Ourselves. We were respectable. We Got the Habit. We saved for a family car. Nichola started calling the spare room the nursery. We were happy.

Tyzacks closed 12th January - left it till then so they didn't ruin Christmas. Last week there we pinched anything we could fit under our coats. All the lads took phones, tools, doorknobs, whatever. Me, there was only one thing I really wanted, apart from my fucking job back.

It was such a big works that we had our own electricity substation. A low brick box topped off with a flat concrete roof and two big grey transformers fenced inside a compound. Once every couple of months a man from the English Electric called round to inspect it. Usually I'd fetch him a cuppa, and while he unlocked the compound and checked over the equipment, we'd chat.

He'd been working for the Electric all his life. His official title was Substation Engineer. He had two thousand on his list, ranging from a few real monsters fed straight from the National Grid down to the hundreds of small ones which supplied a handful of streets or a single factory like Tyzacks. He told me about his job, how when the power came in, the substations stepped it down a stage at a time then filtered it out all over the city. A lethal torrent, harnessed, dammed and diverted, subdued into thousands of tiny streams. I was fascinated.

Tyzacks' substation had a sign on it, they all do. A metal plate enamelled bright yellow. Inside a black triangle, a silhouetted man falling backwards, pinned down by a giant cartoon lightning-bolt like something out of Tom & Jerry. Across the bottom, black capitals said DANGER OF DEATH, only on ours someone had scraped away part of the G so Danger read DANCER. When the works shut down I thought 'right, I'm having that.' I took it home and set it on top of the telly. Nichola thought it was hilarious. She still loved me then.

*

Back at the bus station I pop into the Snacketeria. I get myself a coffee then select a table by the window. The table's bolted to the floor and somebody's carved DARREN FUCKS PIGS into its red Formica surface. I dump my bag of tools by the bench, which is also bolted to the floor, and sit down. Spreading out my list, I cross off Chadwick Road, sip my coffee which tastes okay, and plan my next visit. The caff smells like a hospital. Disinfectant and sick. Unlike a hospital it's almost empty.

An old girl trundles up to my table. Asks if she can join me. She's having a stainless-steel pot of tea for one and a baked potato with grated cheese on top. This is her little treat. The highlight of her day, her week, who knows, her whole flipping life, and she's going to force a conversation.

She glances at my unzipped bag, sees the tools inside and asks me what I do. I do what any decent man in my situation would do. I lie. I tell her I'm a plumber. That's all she needs to hear and now she's off on one, moaning about how cold it's been lately, how pensioners don't get enough to live on these days and how she wishes she could afford central heating. Every time she flaps her mouth her top set of dentures winch down into her gob on cheesy saliva strings, and as she munches her spud, they stick back again, each time with a little more slop underneath.

She begins to dribble and starts banging on about the Common Market, how her daughter married a German and they've got four cars and two double garages outside their detached house. I've no time for this today so I bolt the last of my coffee, pick up my bag, say good-bye and get going. She waves me all the way to the door.

*

The 97 pulls into stand C3. I get on. I pay the man. The bus wallows through town and heads out into a nice bit of suburb. A highly desirable residential area unscathed by strikes or closures. Occasionally the bus pulls over to pick up well preserved ladies in camel coats and Burberry scarves who've left the car at home today and are doing their bit to protect the environment. Ladies who lunch.

Tree-lined crescents and groves, decent shops, pubs that do dinners and correctly-punctuated graffiti. Huge Victorian villas. Places with reception areas, utility rooms, and a woman who does. We slide past one, complete with fairy tale turret, tennis court and a lodge at the entrance to a sweeping gravel drive.

These people don't piss around with gardens - they've got grounds.

I get off at the end of an avenue. The bus stop's immaculate. A shiplap structure which reeks of creosote. Hanging baskets and a notice board for the bridge club. Immediately behind it, down a short tarmac track, is second on the list today.

Montgomery Road. Substation No 1965

Pretty much the same set up as Chadwick Road except the equipment's made by South Wales Switchgear. Clipped laurel bushes inside the fence. The land it's on takes a tiny corner out of four different sets of grounds and four different mansion owners have done their very best to conceal it behind Leylandii, climbing roses and trellis.

I crouch down by the fence, unzip my bag and take out a metal plate. A wave of envy smacks into me. If I had all this I wouldn't hide it away. I'd be straight down to B&Q, get myself a set of the biggest garden floodlights money could buy and shine them straight at it. Then I'd wait until dusk, stretch out on my luxury rattan patio set, sip 200 year old lager from an I Heart Electricity mug and soak up the view, serenaded by the perfect hum of transformers, and dreaming of all that juice blasting out under the streets.

Back in the Snacketeria I get a stainless-steel pot of tea for one and sit at the same table. Darren still Fucks Pigs.

I pour my tea and roll a fag. I can't ever drink tea these days without thinking about work and in particular about Russ. The factory fool. Manufacturing industry's answer to the village idiot.

He'd been there as long as anybody could remember, always the first to turn up in the mornings and the last to go at night.

Russ had the mental age of an eight year old and come to think of it a pretty silly eight year old at that. He must have been in his late fifties and he still lived with his mother. Each and every morning she'd pack him off to work with identical butties, a Mars, and his little tartan flask. A label sewn inside his coat said who he was and where he lived in case he got lost, and the only thing any of us really knew for certain about Russ was that he liked Elvis. He spent his days sweeping up, running errands and helping out in the despatch bay, all the shitty jobs they'd give a scheme lad nowadays.

When management decided to enter us in some daft Chamber of Commerce competition for best kept factory, Russ was given the job of sorting out the tatty flower beds carved out of the knackered turf in front of the Admin block.

He picked up all the litter, dug the beds over and planted them out with bulbs. Contractors were hired in to lay fresh turf.

Russ spent a carefree afternoon leaning on his spade, watching as they laid a level bed of sand, then rolled out the turves and tapped them down flat. Eight o' clock the following morning we clocked in and found Russ sitting in his garden. It looked like a beach. He'd rolled all the turf back up again, stacked it in a neat pile by the entrance, then dug out all the bulbs to see if they were growing. They slabbed it after that.

The best thing about Russ was his teeth. They were shagged. I saw two fall out as he ate his sarnies one break time. He scooped them up, put them in his pocket - probably with all the rest - and carried on munching. He finished up with just the one tooth in the middle, top and bottom. We used to joke about him having central eating.

When the last two dropped out Russ's ma got him fitted up for a set of falsies. He came to work one morning waving a note which he made us all read, bus money and a map.

Today was the big day. The day Russ got his new gob.

12.30 Russ left the factory at the double, hopped on a bus and zoomed off into town.

1.15 He was back and smiling like a horse.

3 o'clock tea break. Russ poured himself a nice hot cup of tea. He took a big gulp and his new dentures started to run down his face - pink goo with white chunks, dripping off his chin and pouring down his overalls.

We held him down till he stopped screaming, then peeled a bit of the pink stuff off his front. Wax.

He'd marched into the dentist's, got so excited he'd grabbed the first thing he saw, bunged a full-size model of some other bugger's mouth into his stupid face and marched out again.

I finish my fag and knock back the rest of the tea. Last on the list today is a monster, a really fucking big one.

*

Back on the bus again and heading through an ex-industrial area. The road very straight with huge factories towering up like the walls of a canyon. All the empty works padlocked, patrolled day and night by security firms. Late middle-aged men - some my mates from Tyzacks - dressed-up in pathetic boys brigade uniforms, working long unsociable hours for lousy pay. Gutted by failure and bored shitless.

Further along the road the factories are already being converted. Ripped apart from the inside, sand blasted, fitted with red toy town window frames then put up for sale as office space that nobody needs.

I get off at a stop in front of a memorial, the names of all the steel workers who pegged it in WW1 listed on a bronze plaque fixed to the remains of the same factory where it was cast. I fetch a wad of steel wool from my tool bag and shine up grandad.

132 thousand volts coming straight off the National Grid via an overhead pylon.

Inside a separate compound, a set of Sealing Ends, each crowned with big ceramic insulators and tapped to neutral earth resistors - huge tanks of distilled water, feed the power through live copper bars to a step-down transformer. The bars sparking and crackling with static in the damp atmosphere. The transformer is oil-cooled with thermostatically controlled fans as backup. It's the size of a terraced house.

The baby ones hum. This fucker thunders.

There's no chance of me getting in here. It's surrounded by tall spiked railings with an electric fence inside that. I wouldn't want to anyway, it scares the shit out of me.

I bolt my plate to the fence, then go home.

*

First Monday morning after Tyzacks went down the toilet I woke, washed, shaved, got dressed as usual and was halfway out the front door before I remembered.

It felt like start of the school holidays all over again. I sat in the kitchen - tea, newspaper and fag as Nichola fussed about, then left for Abbey. After she'd gone I switched on the telly and thought this is the life. I still had all my redundancy money then. I felt like lord of the manor. Lunch time, I met up with a couple of mates who'd also become gentlemen of leisure, and we had a few pints. Tuesday was the same. Come Wednesday teatime I was bored out my skull.

Thursday, thought I'd start on the spare room. Time on my hands and all that. I cleared out all the empty boxes and tea-chests, then pulled the paper off. Horrible thirties stuff, garish crinoline ladies, half-timbered thatched cottages, gaudy wall flowers, oversized bluebirds. Ye Olde Merrie England.

Nichola came back, asked me what did I think I was doing? No chance of that for a good long while she said. No point. Kids cost money. She bustled out. Snapped the latch to on the lavvy door.

I always hated it when she cried.

. I went out with Nichola Friday night. I'd not worked all week but it still felt like, you know, Friday Night. She gave me a right talking to. Said she didn't want a husband who sat in the pub all day. Told me I'd better sort myself out pronto or there'd be trouble, said she'd already spoken to my folks and they were very worried about me. I wouldn't have minded but it'd only been a week.

Next day Nichola finally lost her sense of humour. Acting like Little Miss Snippy Knickers. She cold and efficient. Me a complete idiot. Daggers in her eyes, a very sharp knife in her voice, and long lists of stuff for me to do if I could possibly find the time, fit it into my busy schedule.

Monday morning Nichola took the bus to work and left me the car. I drove into town and signed on - first time in my life and I felt like shit. They took my details, told me I wasn't entitled to anything because of Nichola's income and my pay-off. They asked if I'd considered security work, then gave me a phone number and wished me luck.

I dialled the number from a call-box. It turned out that there were jobs available at, you've guessed it - Tyzacks. I went up there, just out of curiosity really, and found the old place fenced off, a JCB charging around inside. A brand new Portakabin at the gate, all the windows wide open. *Jailhouse Rock* blasting out.

As I pulled in, a man appeared in the doorway. He was wearing a fake policeman's uniform and a white idiot smile. It was Russ.

On the way home I passed a substation. The standard low

brick box with louvered double doors and a flat concrete roof, surrounded by a tall iron fence. The gate was hanging open. I parked up, wandered in, and yanked the sign off.

As a boy I'd always been afraid of substations. Had it drummed into me they were dangerous. Places where bad things happened. My folks told me stories. Kids who went in after kites or footballs and were never seen again. If I saw a substation I'd cross the street to avoid it, not even look at it, so to actually go inside one now, and take something, gave me a real thrill.

I fetched the sign home. Stuck it on top of the telly next to the other one. Nichola got back from Abbey. Told me to get rid of it. I took it out into the shed. That was the real start of my collection.

*

I jolt awake. The couple next door rowing, shagging, then rowing again. I pull the covers over my head. Try to get back to sleep. Each time I start to nod off they're at it again. Eventually I give up, go to the bathroom, clump downstairs and stick the kettle on.

I take my mug through to the shed. I get my tools, the signs and consult my list. They're all local today. I smoke a quick fag and get going.

It's sunny out but freezing. Suddenly I'm busting for a pee. Apart from that I feel okay. I've got 20 quid in my pocket, a new pack of tobacco and something to do. I really miss Nichola, and I know I can't ever undo what's happened, that putting the signs back won't change anything, but at least this way I'm out of the house and busy. All I ever wanted from a job in the first place.

First one today is a bit unusual. The normal brick box - but not fenced off. Plonked on a grassy peninsular at a Y-junction in the road. The station's at the widest point of the Y and at the neck there's a red-brick public toilet which joins onto it. I tighten the last nut and go into the gents. They do say water and electricity don't mix but this is ideal.

Lunch time. I'm dying for a pee again. The only places you can go for one round here are the pubs and they get snotty if you don't buy a drink. I head straight for the nearest. It's a big 50s place with a car park, a family beer garden and a games room. The kind of boozer that does Bingo and a turn at the weekends. I go into the lounge.

The place is covered with red plush, anaglypta and horse brasses except for the actual bar itself which looks like it's been inspired by a Spanish package deal. I order a half, leave the right money on the counter while I go to the gents. Back in the lounge, I take the half over to an alcove and flop down. Pain whacks up my spine. The seats look soft in here, but they feel like concrete.

I roll myself a fag and spark it up. There's the odd time when the novelty of not having a job still appeals. This is definitely one of them. I sip the half and take a look around. There's a fair few blokes my age in here for an early weekday morning which I suppose is typical of this area now, and the odd pensioner - most likely in to keep warm .

When I've finished the half I need a piss again. I go and have one, then get myself a pint. Nichola said she didn't want a man who sat in the pub all day but she's gone now - so who cares?

Pint number three. Nobody's come in, nobody's gone out. Seems like we're all stuck in here for the duration, pissing the day up the wall.

Pint number four. While I'm at the bar a bloke I only knew by sight at Tyzacks emerges from the games room. We greet each other like old mates and he comes over to sit with me. He glances at the tool bag and asks me if I'm working. I tell him not. We leave it at that.

Reminiscing about Tyzacks like it was some fantastic holiday camp-cum-public school, we get onto Russ. I tell him Russ is still there, the only one of us left. Sitting day after day in a sweaty hut parked on the remains of his little garden, with only a new set of teeth and his Elvis tapes for company. We have a laugh about that and he goes off to get the pints in. While he's at the bar it dawns on me I'm just as fucking sad. Worse. He's the first person I've spoken to in almost two weeks. At least Russ has his mum. My folks don't answer the door to me.

The lights flick on. Four o'clock already. How time flies when you're getting leathered. We sink a few more and he asks about the tool-bag again. I'm pissed enough to tell him now, to tell him the truth; I want to tell him the truth, but I mutter something about a mate's car instead and change the subject. We drink up and say good-bye. I stagger home, just make it through the front door, then throw up all over the living room carpet. I crawl upstairs and into bed with my shoes on, over the fence with a wooden ladder, down the other side on a fibre-glass pole, creep across the rose garden and run screaming along a narrow corridor encrusted with glimmering dials and arcing switches.

A semi-circular control room. The Grid Station. Attercliffe. Huge green vitriolite panels map out the nerve system of the city, every substation named, mapped, pinpointed and quantified. Lightning risk levels One, Two & Three.

I enter a vast windowless room, an echoing hollow chamber throbbing with power, pulsing like a monster electro-mechanical heart. The air seethes with energy and I feel my body crackling with fear. The circuit breakers in here are the size of midi-skips, the cables thick as telegraph poles, the busbars heavier than a family car.

I walk into the compound, calmer now, acting like I own the place. It's misty and I can't quite see the top of the first set of sealing ends. The noise is unbelievable. I settle on a concrete wedge bearing a yellow danger sign and roll a fag. Nichola sits beside me. I wish you wouldn't smoke in the house she says and I see a blue halo slide along the first of a set of ten copper HT bars. One by one they all do it. Ten HT bars wrapped in a blue ring of confidence, an inverted gas burner edgeways on and the air thundering with power. Nichola slips her arm around my shoulder. As we kiss I notice a smouldering pink rag sticking out the LV cupboard. An overpowering smell of bacon. I wake up in my clothes. I feel like shit.

I go downstairs and stick the kettle on. I take my mug through to the shed, remember and go back into the house. I open the door to the living room. The stench of rancid beer washes over me. There's sick everywhere. It takes me nearly an hour to clean it all up then I'm ready to go. Instead I sit down on the sofa, the only thing Nichola didn't take. I roll a ciggy.

It was never the signs, they're all the same. Not the list, the electric, the buzz of not getting caught, or the fucking things piling up in the shed.

I had a purpose, a plan. Little trips out with my bag of tools spinning out my useless fag-end of a life. A routine. A way to stop the boredom chewing into my brains. Something to keep my fingers busy.

I feel like it was my fault. I know it wasn't really my fault but I feel like it was. I should have done something, told somebody.

I met the girl on a scruffy bit of grass behind the post office. A nice looking kid with big brown eyes and curly black hair. Pink clothes from head to toe. I suppose she must've been six or seven. She was dressed as Barbie.

She asked what I was up to mister?

I said I worked for the Electric and I was taking the sign away to have it mended.

She asked me where did it come from, the electric. And when it went in the big pipes under the ground could it spill out and hurt the animals that lived in the dirt - rabbits and moles, worms and that?

I said not.

She asked me was it true Jesus died on a hot cross bun?

The day after, and miles away, she turned up again. She was filthy. I asked her what she was doing. She said she was having an adventure.

Next time I saw her was on the news.

She'd been burnt to death.

I pick up my tool bag from the living room floor where I dropped it last night.

I walk over to Shirland Lane.

Shirland Lane Substation No. 3009

A brand new spiked fence with three big yellow danger signs. I bolt mine back with the others. A mountain of rotting flowers. This is where it happened.

I'd visited this one a couple of days before the accident - which is where I first met the Barbie girl - and it was open. Kids break in sometimes to keep warm, smoke fags, drink cider. They'd pulled the door off the LV cupboard.

I should have reported it, taken two minutes away from my stupid list, my pathetic substitute for a job, a life, and I might have saved her, but I didn't.

Two days later she wandered in. The poor little sod fell against the contacts.

Me and Nichola were sat watching the news. By this time I was meant to be working days as a security guard at Tyzacks - just till something decent turned up, but I wasn't. I was out everyday with my tools and the fucking list.

The little girl's picture flashed onto the screen. There was a report on the accident. Ashen-faced residents saying how dreadful it was, how when it happened all the power went off, and a woman from the Electric saying there'd be a full inquiry.

They stuck a camera in the mother's face. Asked her how she felt. She went berserk.

Nichola stood up, took the sign off the telly, walked through to the kitchen and slammed the door.

I went in after her. Found her bent over the sink, elbows on the drainer. The sign pressed to her forehead. Tears streaming onto the dirty pots. I put my arms round her. Kissed the back of her neck. As my lips touched she spun round, and with make-up climbing down her face Nichola slashed at me with the sign. In all she must've hit me twenty or thirty times before she ran out of steam. I stood there taking it and waiting for her to stop, each blow felt like the end of something, as if she was driving nails back into one of the tea chests in the spare room, packing up what little was left between us all ready for the binmen.

Next day I went into town, drew all my redundancy money out the bank and put it in an envelope.

I took a bus to the estate. I found the house, no problem. It was close by Shirland Lane substation and easy to spot. The ruched lacy curtains shut tight and the front garden piled high with flowers - bouquets, wreaths and a giant Barbie made from pink and white carnations. I picked my way up the block-paved driveway and shoved the envelope through the letterbox.

When Nichola got back from Abbey I told her everything.

Promised I'd put all the signs back. Nichola knew about them anyway. Said she'd seen them piled up in the shed and guessed I wasn't working.

She left me.

*

Three to go. Two I missed out yesterday and DANCER OF DEATH. I get the bus up to Tyzacks. The gate's wide open.

It's gone. Bulldozed flat. Nothing left except the substation, and they're knocking that down. I watch through the fence as demolition men forklift big grey English Electric transformers onto a low loader.

A JCB moves in, smashes up the concrete base, then digs a massive pit for all the rubble. Russ appears in the doorway of the Portakabin. He's waving a teapot. Everybody knocks off and goes inside.

Tyzacks; Little London Road. Substation No 1849

I go in through the gate, stumbling across broken concrete. I drop my stuff and stand in the shattered guts of substation No 1849.

Silence.

The air tastes of diesel. I feel alone and useless.

RETURN TO SENDER erupts from Russ' Portacabin. I pick up my tool bag, my list and the last three signs. Then I chuck the fuckers into the pit.

The Shadow Man

Stephen Wade

'I'm going to do something significant.' he vowed. And that's how he came to have the 'appointment with destiny'.

He was a member of the shadow people. One of those who worked dutifully to keep family, home and car functioning without imbalance or upset. He was content as a machine is content once all parts are oiled and operating satisfactorily. After all, he had been reminded continually since little boy status, there were waifs starving in Africa who would welcome his pie-crusts and oily gravy. And there was no point in moaning about injustice. What you did was persevere.

So he joined the shadows, stepping into their microcosm of bland cafes and Ford Fiestas, of bills clustered behind the mantel-clock and package-deal holidays in the disenchantments of sun and litter.

He had his initials stuck on his Samsonite briefcase and his official name was placed on his office door. The computer comforted him with e-mails and the phone rang at regular intervals. Lunch was sandwiches and flask; entertainment was peeping out of the shadows and the randy, shameless world of sex and heartbeats, vows and regrets. The shreds of passion filled the air about him like motes in sunlight, and his gaze went freely to glossy wank-mag images of young limbs and full breasts.

'It'll be something grand that I do. Something that will bring me to notice. Something that just isn't me. Not criminal, not seedy. A gesture against all this. A great yell at the light we all know is there inside, but we walk on, heads down, scared.'

There were moments when he thought of missed opportunities for passion. But then he said the words and smiled. It came nowhere near to the reality. Reality was stone walls but dreams were sawdust. In the office it was always difficult. They laughed at him, and he knew it. He lingered outside doors after leaving a room, just to hear the truth.

'Dennis... he's got a problem..'

'Yeah. Dennis.'

(Sniggers).

'What he needs is a long holiday...'

'What he needs is a good shag.'

There was one time when, sitting close to a young woman in the office at a more-than-usually boring meeting, he had come close to opening the prison door and letting the warmth of his needing fill him. He had been aroused by her perfume, and he was compelled to look furtively at her womanly neck and fine dark hair. Then the sensual geometry of angled straps and the fastenings of her bra beneath the flimsy cream blouse. His gaze wandered to her hands. The long, creaturely fingers, made for kissing. How like living beings they were, ready to clasp, mark, caress and dig into flesh. She had turned once, just a quick glance of knowing, as if his eyes had cut into her. But he gave a bland smile and pretended to investigate the cartridge of his fountain pen.

My revolt is going to be nothing to do with guns or bombs but it will change things.

He said this into his coffee-cup.

And so he kept merging into shadows. Something forced him to stay outside any impassioned debate. In the office, colleagues would sometimes discuss the latest horrific murder. Someone had perhaps strangled a tiny tot. Hmmm. Awful. One should feel outrage of course.

Their faces would stare - Deirdre, Gavin, Sandra - fix on him blankly, like when you wait for a chimp at the zoo to swing on a rotten log for your entertainment. Yeah. They wanted him to fall into the jungle shit, just for them. For their little lives.

'What do you think, Dennis?'

'Have you any thoughts on this, Dennis?'

He would work up the perfunctory grimace on the dead face and cultivate the meaningless nod. He had a special nod of the head which signalled his presence in the conversation: his vague involvement. Yet the face betrayed nothing of the indifference within.

Yes, what I'm going to do is like the chick cracking through the beautiful pale-blue egg into the first sky. Into the first sounds and colours.

'So you don't believe in capital punishment then, Dennis?'

'No, Sandra. No. It's barbaric...'

He played to the approving smiles like a clown to the gallery. It was a comfort to be approved of, but inside his guts twisted and wrenched into a rock of hatred that would explode one day.

'See, Dennis talks sense. Doesn't say much. But still waters run deep.'

Things were not made easier by the letters that started arriving from a Mr Zygmunt Osvik, refugee from war-torn Poland. Mr Osvik mixed autobiography with accounts of his experience of the current taxation system as applied to small businessmen such as himself. The Shadow Man kept all the letters. He took them home and stored them in a special folder. They were works of literature, to his mind at least.

Dear Anonymous Clerk,

I write to you as a man poor in pounds sterling but rich in my spirit. I communicate poems to you, from a heart soaked in the waters of forgetting. But my heart cannot forget those I have lost, and my pain here in exile is worsened by your outrageous demands for back-payments of monies. Lucre is the detritus we have to sit on, so we can sing about a heaven free of bargaining.

Yours,

Zygmunt Osvik.

The Shadow Man had tried, genuinely tried, to somehow make contact with this enigmatic world of supposed caring and sharing. He had read the right books. For a few years, he dutifully bought the Booker Prize short-listed novels and fixed like a ravenous rat on the fascinating ambiguities of style; on the displays of post-modern allusion; on the fancy rhetoric such works appeared to encourage. The frustration of trying to enter these odd modes of thought drove him to rap the table. He started learning languages instead. On the bus to work he would learn lists of Spanish words and memorise them. He spent longer in cafés, just sitting and making lists in a cheap notebook.

'I am going to be cosmopolitan and sit at café tables al fresco.'

His café life led to a slightly embarrassing moment. At the Happy Albion, the place he frequented for peace of mind and anti-stress therapy of listening to small-talk and sipping creamy coffee, he had read a particular sentence in one of these intellectual volumes. The author had written of a woman professor: *'Kate, as with all of us, knew the foolish call of Prufrock's mermaids, and walked on, nevertheless, into the same tired days.'*

This maddened The Shadow Man because he had no idea who Prufrock was. Why write that? Why lose the reader? After all, the stupid author was supposed to be telling a story.

Apparently it was a story. This author was making a story into something to undermine, even to dismantle, everything you knew. But he still felt the rage, and his palm came down on the mock-Tudor table: the mock-oak, mock-English breakfast board of Happy Albion.

'You all right mate?' the chubby owner yelled at him, looking across as he buttered a teacake.

'Yes, sorry. Sorry.'

Heads turned of course. There were nervous smiles. But there was a silence like a crematorium lawn. The Shadow Man did his nod. He wanted a smile but all that happened was the nod.

He thought more often of Zygmunt Osvik and his songs made to a lonely and high roof, all in an alien land. He knew that alien land, The Shadow Man. He knew it could be made by cars in the drive and families around the television. Once he had lived there he left. He never went there again.

'I'm going to make everyone think again. Stop them all being stuck like me. I'm going to have the impact of a child at a serious meeting. I'm to be a puck, a gadfly.'

This realisation came one day when The Shadow Man opened his eyes to the real facts about people. They were all living like him. The isolation so many had to bear was heroic, and the only release, it seemed to him in his dark vision, was the bottle and the needle. It was just that some were talented actors and had a wider range of gestures, ploys, devices, dodges and lies than he did. What really brought this home to him was the latest letter from Mr Osvik of Forley. Mr Osvik made it clear that he had a large grudge against the bureaucrats.

Dear Mr Taxman,

I hope you are happy now that you have ruined me. I have worked for this country since escaping the Nazis, and served you well. What do you reward me with? Huge taxation dues and unbearable burdens simply because I prospered a little, using my craft of bookbinder. Words, words, words, my dear people. You kill them, like you put knife into soul of poem and call it finance. I spit on your finance. Finance is murdering poetry in this country. In all country.

Yours…

So it went on, letters arriving day after day from this literate, lonely man adrift among his books and papers, feeling a grievance at his adopted country. The Shadow Man felt a kindred spirit. His destiny was going to be words. He too would write letters. He would revolt by filling the world of Mr Osvik and those like him, with colour.

In the market one weekend he strolled aimlessly around, gazed with the usual vacancy at discarded jewellery, cheap radios and lines of tools showing men what their work should be. He liked the smell, though. The rotten fruit, the wet fish, the pipe tobacco. He liked to sit on the benches around the central 'wishing-well' – a tiled, coin-littered pond, like a miniature swimming pool. He liked to watch the urchins, their noses snuffling up against the sweet counters. That weekend though, he saw something different - a sight as alluring as a Persian bazaar to his tired city stare: a stall selling wooden stamps with all kinds of designs, and little square ink-pads. There were kangaroos, bears, stars, boats. You could stamp their shapes on paper and write messages or greetings. He saw children playing with them, composing poems and loving words with little pictures of rainbows and animals. This chance episode turned his life around.

That Monday, his fellow clerks saw him apply himself to paperwork with more alacrity and enthusiasm. He even grinned at one point. After a few hours of pure concentration the letter to Mr Osvik was done. He watched the mailing clerk approach and he saw all the formal letters go in the bag. Piles of official blue and white envelopes, card envelopes with weighty documents; packages with wads of paper; final demands with formidable black ink on the cover. On top of this he placed his letter. The mail clerk stopped and looked at it. His eyes looked quizzically at The Shadow Man. He paused, breath smelling faintly of beer. Clearly, pink with cartoons of taxmen doing ridiculous things like playing darts in a seedy pub or picking their noses with pencils was not really acceptable. But the Shadow Man put his finger to his lips. A pint was promised.

The mail went.

A few days passed as normal. The Shadow Man went on the usual round of window-shopping. He sat in the café and filled in his notebook. He learned his list of Hebrew words and the names of the Leeds United players in Don Revie's best team. He improved himself intellectually as always. But he dressed differently. Everything was to be bohemian now. In lunch breaks he had some body-piercing done and his hair cropped very short. Even the obligatory grey or black suits went to

Oxfam and he began to wear white and cream jackets and trousers, with a scarf or a cravat. If he wore a tie, it was very loud. He became something of a *flaneur*. He had read that certain French poets became *flaneurs* back in the nineteenth century, which had meant walking slowly and taking in the sounds and movements of the world. They ignored time completely. They took time to observe and to talk.

Naturally, his colleagues noticed these outward changes, and talked of him when he was out of the room.

'So, he *is* gay. I always had a feeling...'

'A ha... our friend has come out. It was that tangerine jacket and the nose-piercing that convinced me.'

'He wants to watch it. He'll be asked to step upstairs to floor twenty and questioned about his appearance. After all, this *is* the Inland Revenue.'

The Shadow Man walked into the office one afternoon and Mr. Pierce was there. Mr Pierce from the top desk. He was talking about a strange phone call he had.

'From a client. A Mr Osnachek or something. Says he had a beautiful letter from us. Says, in fact, it was a poem. A work of art. Can you believe that? Art from the Inland Revenue!'

'I know that name...' Sandra frowned. 'Ah yeah... Mr Osnik. He's nuts. An Auschwitz survivor. If you check the files, there's about a million letters from him. Usually moaning.'

They all sniggered. Mr Pierce laughed again, glanced once over to The Shadow Man, then returned to the coffee-soaked den in his lofty heights. The Shadow Man smiled inside and wrote another letter, adorned with his stamps and little cartoons.

It went on for weeks. He put art and joy into as many lives as possible with his coloured stamps and colourings. His collection grew. He bought camel - shapes and rabbit figures. Then he moved on to trying drawings of his own and found that he liked it. From time to time he showed his caricatures to Sandra or to Gavin. They cracked a wrinkle politely, to humour him of course. Good boy. Carry on. You're harmless. One of them actually said: 'No-one could harm you - you're like a kid.'

But his work was coming on well. He bought a book on how to do cartoons and caricatures. He practised in the Happy Albion and at lunch times. He concentrated so hard that he found himself with his tongue sticking out of his mouth like some school kid. Then he chuckled and was aware that people were watching him again.

At last his chance came. The Shadow Man, well known in the office for his powers of written expression, was asked to write and distribute a letter to clients, explaining what tax people did. He should try to make them sound human, making it clear that tax officers were family men and women, with hobbies, with lives. So he started work, determined to use all his new-found skills with shape and colour, mixing word and image. As instructed he set out to destroy the stereotype of his colleagues being stuffy and boring. It was a PR exercise, after all.

The Shadow Man stayed late after working hard on his letter all day, printing it out and duplicating it himself. He wanted to make sure that his mail went out that evening. He did everything himself after sending the mail-clerk off for a 'coffee break' - which meant a few hours in the pub nearby. He locked the door of the post-room, made some tea, put a Mozart string quartet on his portable CD player, and settled down. All he had to do was fold the leaflets and tuck them neatly in a standard envelope, being careful to match the printed address with the envelope-window. It was a menial, robotic task but he loved it. His own creative work was being sent to an initial batch of one thousand people; in this case all employees of Ludford City Transport - renowned gossips and trouble-stirrers. Every time he slotted one in an envelope he saw his artwork and felt a thrill of satisfaction.

The scene was a Roman orgy in a cartoon frieze. There was Sandra being buggered by Mr Pierce. Gavin was on the loo, reading Whips and Leather Gear. Old Deirdre was stuffing tissues into her bra while being groped by a toy-boy. He had everybody there, copulating or lending a lewd and helping hand: the filing clerks, the counter staff, the Tax Officers Higher Grade who were in flowery underwear and punk slave-rings. It was the office party of the decade, pornographic scenes unknown in Taxation history. And all this in technicolour, blazed beneath the dull letterhead of that usually depressingly unwelcome sheet of Inland Revenue paper. He had written some predictable lines about the thrills of taxation as a career, and about the amazing rapport between the staff. How they had rich, full lives and a range of fulfilling pastimes. And there, beneath it all, in glorious tri-colour script, was the artist's name: The Shadow Man.

He brushed the seal of the last envelope along the sponge-tray, placed all the envelopes in delivery sacks, and left a noted instruction for the mail-sorter. He walked along a series of long deserted corridors until he reached the landing by the lift. He thought of those two bulky hessian sacks awaiting that red GPO van.

'Yes, I did it. My work… dropping through mail-boxes. Painting the town red… sort of.'

The Shadow Man savoured the wonderful moment. As he stepped into the lift, a sneaky little smile of anticipation flickered on his face. His appointment with destiny had arrived.

The Cold

C John Roberts

In hindsight, all these years later, it seems so absurd. Absurd that something as simple as a cold one October weekend could so disturb the order of my waking life. For certainly the incident I am about to recount can only have been the product of my own feverish mind.

You must have known that sickness in which you can be hot and cold at the same time. A burning within the bones shoots along twisted miles of nerve and into your skull, while your skin feels like cold, damp stone, sweat drying upon you with the consistency of cling film, wrapping you up nice and tight. My mind raced, unable to settle to any single line of thought, desperate to outrun that gnawing fever. My eyes were weeping and sore from wiping and rubbing. My throat stung so that I would gag in trying to hold back a painful cough. Even the sounds of the world seemed to warp and ring with a dull echo. This was how it started, I suppose

All these symptoms left me isolated, confined within an aching body that hardly seemed to be mine. Like most men, I have never been very good at dealing with illness, especially my own. It might only have been a cold but to me it was a bitter spirit gnawing through to the marrow. The heat of the electric fire seemed artificial, masking rather than replacing the cold that seeped in beneath the door of my ill-kept basement flat. It was the evening of a miserable Friday, spent in the company of an old radio that filled me and the room with the sickly sweet drivel of our local station, peppered by the occasional crackle of static. A thick mist had settled over the world beyond my window and the humming in my ears masked any sound from the road or park opposite. Even the everyday sounds of people conducting their lives in the surrounding flats, something I usually considered an annoyance, had faded away to distant scratching. A claustrophobic panic gathered slowly around me as I faced the prospect of another evening alone. I had to get out for a while, whatever the weather.

With my coat pulled tight I stepped out into the frigid air. The park I live beside once formed the grounds of Cohn House; a long abandoned Georgian mansion. Those carefully sculptured gardens had once been the buffer zone to keep the reality of the surrounding urbanisation of Victorian town houses at a distance. Now, its urban status as a council maintained park was clearly marked out by the abundance of crisp packets and crushed beer cans littering the paths. The aura of decay that permeated the park appealed to me that evening, and so I crossed the road and passed through the rusting gate opposite.

It was late autumn and already the sky was turning black. The infrequent lighting throughout the park failed to reveal much beyond the patch of gravel and mush of leaves directly under my feet, but at least I did not have to walk in the pitch black. Perhaps I would have welcomed darkness for any amount of light seemed to glare and hurt my eyes. The air was cold, crisp and very still. I knew the park well and did not need to pay much attention to where my feet fell or where they took me. I recall the dark outlines of familiar trees and the vague humming sounds from the roads that enclose the park. I could hear laughter from the car park of the local restaurant as a man and woman clung to one another while fumbling for the key to his car. That could have been me. I belonged to this world; led a civilised if mostly impoverished twenty-something lifestyle. A few drinks and a quick meal followed by an easy lay and that awkward, permanent parting. I suppose I was a solitary figure even then. Perhaps I would have become the recluse I am regardless of the events of that night. But I had my routines, my way of dealing with the world. All I have accomplished is the turning of a feverish fantasy into this justification for an empty life. I wonder if that man felt any warmth for the woman he hugged there beside the car, or if it was simply received. I wonder if he found his own excuses for growing old alone.

With the cool air and occasional breeze easing the tightness in my chest I ambled on along one of my favourite paths - the one that leads around the side of the mansion where the ground rises steeply and the path involves a flight of worn sandstone steps. My mind was split in two, half watching my feet as they climbed each step in turn, half turned inwards to a similarly miserable debate about my place in this dilapidated city. Preoccupied, I did not notice the old couple approaching from the opposite direction until they were quite near. What they were discussing I do not know, although the question has obsessed me ever since. Had it not been for my cold, perhaps I would have heard more. As for a description, all I can say is that I believe the old man had an accent, perhaps that of a Polish immigrant. I remember raising my head and smiling as they walked by, for the old always seem so afraid of the young. They seemed so engrossed in their conversation that I doubt they even knew I was there. The old man was speaking energetically, as though sharing some great discovery or imparting some wisdom of incalculable value.

'And so these theories,' he was saying, 'if they prove to be correct may give my fears...' It was here that I lost my hold on his voice as they walked by me into the darkness and began to descend the steps I had just climbed.

For some reason I felt an urge to walk back to the top of the steps and catch sight of them again. The old man's words intrigued me as, no doubt, he wished they would his wife. Hoping, perhaps, to entice her to step across into his own interior world by conveying to her something of his own enthusiasm. But the way she walked with her head inclined slightly towards her husband didn't fit this theory. This was not the distant manner of a woman enduring the preaching of her husband to maintain the peace. It occurred to me that she was more than simply his wife of long and overly familiar standing. Over the years they had grown so alike, knowing each other so intimately, that it would be astute to regard them as a single being. A bonding that reached beyond the purely religious or state sanctioned contract. They had completed that quest which an exchange of rings marked the beginning of, and not the end.

I walked on along the gravelled path, my feverish mind repeating the old man's misplaced words over and over. 'And so these theories... if they prove...' They swirled about me, refusing to be forgotten and causing me to dwell upon the brief image I had glimpsed of those strangers' lives. I followed the path beside a grove of sapling oak trees that had been planted years before I was born, until I emerged by the lake at the heart of the park.

A mist had begun to rise, glowing faintly orange under the neon of the park and city lights. A glow that revealed the surface of the water by reflecting in the pattern of ripples which fluttered there. I could feel a chill moisture in the air and upon my lungs, causing me to cough and splutter. But as I looked upon the peacefulness of the scene before me I knew I would risk the worsening of my cold to claim some of its calm for myself. I took to the path along the edge of the lake, my head turned slightly to the left so I could gaze out across the waters and permit the dancing of the ripples to entertain me. For a time I knew nothing, other than the companionship of the lake and the steady fall of my feet upon the path. My eyes were hardly focused and my hands grew steadily more numb in my pockets. I walked like this for a long time before I became aware of a noise in the distance.

At first I took no notice as the sound had a regular pattern - a distant echoing screech which in its frequency seemed to agree with the harmony of the lights as they played upon the surface of the lake. The final note of each grinding screech was overlapped by the echo of the screech before, breaking the sound down into an all purpose static that mingled with the sounds of the water splashing against the uneven rim of the lake. But as the noise grew nearer and its echo weaker I thought I could see a silhouette some short distance around the curving edge of the lake. The outline of two figures and some object I couldn't quite make out was moving toward me.

Drawing closer, the two silhouettes slowly resolved into the forms of a young man and a woman. I stood unseen as yet, the park lights not revealing much through the mist. Their attention was held by the object before them which, judging by its shape, could only be an old fashioned pram. This pram rocked slowly back and forth on its four wheels, squeaking each time that it was pushed. They came around the lake edge until I stood quite close to them. I noted how cautiously I had begun to move, as though to be seen by them would be a grave mistake. I had made no conscious decision to spy upon this young couple and yet now found myself doing just that. Somehow it seemed that I knew these people. Something of their gestures and the timid, almost fragile way in which they slid the soles of their feet upon the gravel, as though afraid they might fall. A faint breeze picked up to caress the frigid airs and tickle at the back of my throat. For a moment I thought I would gag as I fought to stifle my cough. Then as the breeze passed me I heard some portion of what they were discussing. So intent was I not to miss a single word, as I had with the old couple before, that I believe I even risked moving a step or two closer.

The woman spoke: 'No Abel, this must not endure; we are committed…' but then the breeze grew stronger. The sudden wind seemed to sever me from the couple, placing a barrier between us. It was then as I stepped back away from them and the edge of the lake that it dawned on me why I was so interested in these two. Their gestures and their words seemed so odd, so out of place or even time. I felt certain then, if only for a moment, that they had cause to fear falling, and the risk to brittle bones that a fall would entail. For surely here before me was that same but no longer old couple I had passed earlier. It seems insane that I should have thought so, but there and then beside that lake, shivering, it seemed so clear, so obvious. The years had fallen away from them to reveal the strong firm bodies of their youth, yet possessed still by the caution of the old. For a moment I stood transfixed, but the next sound was to bring me a reminder of the normal world in which I lived. Carried to me upon the breeze I heard the guileless laughter of the infant within its pram. No doubt it gazed out upon the shimmering ripples on the lake and found them pleasing, much as I had done. I smiled at my own bizarre and morbid turn of thought, resolving then to leave this couple and their child undisturbed where they stood, all admiring the beauty of the lake. I pushed my hands deep into my pockets, bowed my head so that my chin was tucked firmly under the collar of my coat, then stepped out and walked quickly by. They were standing silently, looking down upon their child. Each of them seemed lost within their own private thoughts, and this was how I left them.

As I passed through the gate at the top of the park I believe I heard the wheels of the pram squeak once more as they rocked it gently back and forth, no doubt to ease their child into sleep. Although as I continued upon my way I could not help but remember how near those front wheels had been to the stones upon the edge of the lake. I had half turned the key in the lock to my front door when I heard the final sound. A splashing of water in the near distance. It could have been an otter diving into the water, or a bird taking a fish, or any number of similar innocent things. I do not remember leaving the door to my flat half open, or how long it took me to race my way back to that place by the water's edge. I know that when I arrived my legs were so weak that I tumbled and slipped, almost cracking my own skull on the lake's stony rim. For a while I gulped at the air, desperate to be rid of the pain in my chest, waiting for my thoughts to become clear.

Slowly, I raised my head and looked out across the water. I saw no otter, duck or swan upon the surface. The couple had gone, as I knew they would have. Only the lake itself seemed less at ease than myself. That pattern of ripples reflecting the lights through the thinning mist seemed much disturbed.

Savage Words

Stephen Mawson

The alarm rang at eight thirty pm and Jennifer punched the clock into the corner of the room as quickly as she could. Quietly, she slipped out of bed, leaving Carl to sleep a while longer. She shuffled down the creaking stairs to the kitchen. The kitchen and living room was actually one long room separated roughly by different decor. The kitchen had a dirty but practical look while the living room aimed for that 'yuck' kind of response. And in between the two rooms, like a roadblock, was the desk.

Jennifer was just nineteen, and very practical. She lit the coal fire beside the desk first, then fixed herself some breakfast. She ate strawberry jam on toast and drank coffee from the huge jar she'd prepared for Carl. When she'd finished she prepared the desk. She laid out fresh paper, emptied the ashtray, and polished the spot at the right hand side of the type writer.

When her jobs were done, Jennifer sat at the desk and fed a fresh piece of paper into the typewriter. She stroked her fingers over the keys, her heart racing and her lips quickly going dry. A bright, white light from the solitary light bulb above threw shadows over her face and made her look holy. She breathed deep and ran her fingers through her hair. A pile of unused paper sat to the left of the typewriter but the finished writing always ended up in the fireplace... always.

As Carl walked into the room Jennifer stood up quickly and backed away from the desk.

'Will you write again today?' she asked.

He drew back the curtains, letting the amethyst sunlight flood in. The clock on his desk blinked nine zero nine pm. He said, 'I don't think I have a choice Jen, do you?'

Jennifer licked her lips and advanced upon the fridge. It was an ordinary looking upright appliance; ordinary in every way except for how it was being used. The fridge was the only clean thing in the house and its white mass looked out of place on the grimy living room carpet. When she opened its door and the light came on, the smell of disinfectant burst out and filled the room for a while. Cleaning and disinfecting the fridge was another one of Jennifer's responsibilities.

The fridge was empty save for one full, white carrier bag. Jennifer carried the bag over to the desk where Carl was waiting. She used one hand to hold the handle and the other to support its weight. She placed the bag on the floor in front of the desk and opened it up. A putrid smell fled the bag, making her squirm. She took out the head and carefully placed it on the desk beside the typewriter. The head slipped a little on the polished wood there, then it settled with its mouth and eyes closed tight.

Carl sat watching her as he lit a cigarette. Jen always enjoyed this part, he could tell. He played up to her though. His old office swivel chair was tilted back to the fullest and he held a moody stare on the girl through his smoke. He couldn't help his eyes wandering over her body. A faint aroma of strawberry constantly surrounded her, but only someone who knew her well would know that it wasn't that perfume she smelled of, but sweets. And this young, feisty, sexually-active woman was infatuated with him.

Being mysterious isn't hard he thought. *It isn't hard at all.*

He watched her place the calf's head on the desk then light the open fire by his side. He sat and smoked while the fire grew and the room warmed. She hadn't taken her eyes off of him the whole time. Her chest heaved up and down in excitement. He was ready. Now.

The typewriter was an antique, heavy Remington – a black monstrosity that had been so thoroughly used over so many years that no letters remained on the keys. In his secret heart Carl knew he couldn't possibly write a decent thing in real life, but on this heap of scrap he was Shakespeare. *Shakespeare,* he thought as he rubbed his unshaved chin.

He depressed the first key and Jennifer let out a little squeak. He began to type, slowly at first, then faster. Jen had once said that it sounded like an old steam train gaining speed but without the steam. That clack clack clacking building up into a machine gunning barrage of clicks.

Gradually Carl slipped into that place where writers go when they write. He remembered that someone had once said, *'I am not a writer except when I write'.* Carl liked that quote but rather thought he himself would have said *'I am not alive except when I write'*.

Fifteen minutes into the session and the calf's head twitched. It had squinted its brow slightly. Carl stopped and Jennifer jumped up from beside the fire. They looked at each other, Carl's lips curling slightly into a smile, Jen's face beaming up in girlish glee. He yanked the page from the typewriter and threw it in the fire. Jennifer took a page from the fresh pile and fed it into the machine. He began again.

Moments later and the twitching started again. Carl tapped away furiously, his face twisted into pure concentration, sweat beading upon his brow.

'Cig Jen,' he croaked.

She jumped up on his command and placed one in his mouth. He raised his head a little while she held the match to the cigarette. He puffed blue smoke over the keys, then the head opened its mouth. A slight whisper of air left its mouth. The page was burned and a fresh page started. Carl typed until sunrise. Jennifer waited until sunrise. Then they slept.

Later, Jennifer sat at the typewriter, as excited as ever. From here she could see the whole living room. A room that was not really for living in. The blinds had to be left closed all the time in case someone should see in, and the one light bulb that lit the room made it feel cold and unwelcoming. On the left of the room stood the fridge, the stereo and a spider plant that was dying a slow, dehydrating death. The whole opposite wall was taken up by rusty grey lockers that Carl had stolen one night from a disused factory, transporting them away in his van. Each individual locker was padlocked, and neatly labeled. This labeling was another of Jennifer's responsibilities and she was proud of her work. From the top left the labels read DOG, then CAT, next GOAT and so on - a catalogue of other heads they had worked on. *So many failures*, she thought, slowly shaking her head. As proud as Jennifer was, she was also a little jealous. Why couldn't she make the magic work? *Wasn't fair. Wasn't fucking fair one bit.* She'd tried while Carl was asleep, tapping away quietly. She'd tried to make the heads twitch just a little, just a tiny, tiny bit but she couldn't do it. She got bored easily and couldn't concentrate.

Things had been getting tense around the house lately. Carl was feeling a failure, and Jennifer was idolizing him less. He could make the magic work, but couldn't make it do what he wanted. Worst of all he couldn't open their eyes. The fawn's head nearly did... once. But it shrieked such an awful scream that neither of them could stand it, and they had to burn the thing. They *had* to burn it even though it was their biggest success. And now they tried again every night, each time with a different head, until they both felt useless and tired. Then they'd fuck and go to sleep.

Carl came in and Jennifer turned to him from the desk.

'Should I get it?'

'What do you think, Jen?'

He lit a smoke and rummaged through the cupboards for something to eat. Spaghetti hoops, spaghetti bolognaise, Alphabetti Spaghetti, strawberry pop tarts... Jennifer had been shopping. Carl stuck two pop tarts in the toaster and slopped some spaghetti bolognaise into a pan. When his food was ready he put it all in one bowl and ate it at the desk. It was hot, it tasted good, but it was still spaghetti bolognaise and pop tarts.

Jennifer watched Carl eat with fascination, and when he'd finished and started on a cup of coffee, she fetched the head. Things may have not been going to plan but the lust she had for him hadn't faltered. He had a power, a mysteriousness, that made her feel electric and plugged in. She lugged the bag over to the typewriter.

'We're going to need a new one soon, this one's starting to

stink big time,' she said as she screwed up her nose like a little rabbit. It was a little thing but it showed how young she was, and Carl felt guilty for a moment. Just a moment. Then the moment was passed. He fixed his gaze on the head. Its closed eyes mocked, and its sinking flesh repulsed him. He hated the thing and he cursed the farmer who had bred it.

Getting the heads was becoming hard work. They would snatch the animals from houses, farms, animal refuges and once even a zoo. They never killed them until they got them home. Carl had a tranquiliser gun, and a shot from that usually kept them quiet until they'd done. In the back yard, the two of them would wait for the animal to wake up and struggle in its bonds. Then Jennifer would watch with excitement as Carl sat on the drugged animal and sawed its living head off into an old steel bath.

At the desk, Carl began. He was going for it tonight. He had no plans to stop until the calf opened up its eyes.

'No fucking around tonight Jen,' he said, 'We're going for it tonight. No shit at all.'

Jennifer giggled and jumped up and down on the spot, ready to blow at any second. She took out two cigarettes and lit them both, placing one in Carl's mouth. Over in the corner of the room was a beat-up, old stereo. She pulled out a dusty vinyl record from under the couch and put it on loud. She had chosen The Doors, and as the songs built up into its frenzy, so did Jennifer's dance. At first her dancing had distracted Carl a little, but by the climax of the last song she was shambling and jumping around. By then Carl was far into that 'other place'.

When the head twitched for the first time Jennifer didn't see it because she was simulating oral sex on a bar of chocolate beside the fire, but she saw the page fly past her into the fire and flicker up in smoke. She spun and rose to the typewriter to put in another sheet for Carl, who was lighting another smoke.

He began again as soon as she'd done, humming away to what was the fifth album of the night. But when the mouth actually did open Jennifer was there and she cried out aloud, 'Get the fuck in... I said get right the fuck in!' She ran around the room in near hysterics.

Carl typed like a man possessed, sometimes jamming the keys from the speed. His hair was damp from the sweat; he kept running through it with his fingers. He felt damn good tonight and he was sure the eyes would open. They just *had* to open. It had never been this good. And Jen had never run around the room in such excitement before.

Around half past five in the morning the mood was different. The fire was dying and Jennifer was asleep on the couch. The head had done nothing more for hours but Carl hadn't slowed. His fingers ached and creaked with the strain. Outside it was starting to get light again. Soon he would have to sleep, and he would know then for sure that he was never going to open their eyes, any of them. He stood up and slammed his hands down on the desk. He leaned over to the head.

'Open your fucking eyes, goddamn you.'

Jennifer awoke, suddenly startled by the shouting.

The calf's jaw slacked open, corners dribbling, and it screamed. A high, gibbering scream that shook and shrieked into Carl's face. He fell back into his chair with his hands over his ears. His guts rumbled and his teeth vibrated at the sound. Jennifer sat up quickly and tried to squirm further away from the noise, but to where? *That noise!* It was all going wrong.

Carl, usually terrified by the screaming, suddenly didn't care. He sat forward and began to type along with the screeching. He typed as fast as his aching fingers would allow him. The scream quietened for a while, eventually trailing off to a whisper. The eyelids relaxed. The eyes opened slowly. Silently.

And Carl watched.

The eyelids dragged open. From where she was sitting, Jennifer could only see the back of the head, but the fear made her stay put. Carl realized this, but didn't speak. He just stared at those opening eyes. The smoke rose up from his cigarette. And it was working. The lids slipped upward. The world was still. Carl got what he wanted. Carl got nothing. The lids opened to holes of nothingness. Dead eyes. Dead, ignorant, blank eyes like jelly. Black jelly with no life, no intelligence and no promise. Carl screamed and gibbered and wailed. He slumped back in his chair and looked over at Jennifer, who was trying to burrow into the couch. Then the screaming stopped.

After a few minutes Jennifer rose slowly from the chair and walked over to the desk where Carl was struggling to breathe. She didn't know what to say. Carl clutched at his chest, a terrible pain eating him alive. The shock of the eyes was drawing the life out of him and he struggled to speak.

'Fuck Shakespeare,' he groaned.

Then he died.

Jennifer smoked a cigarette and watched sunrise, then slept.

The next night she sat at the desk. She had done all her jobs, then bathed; scrubbed all clean. Her heart raced and her lips began to dry. A pile of plain paper sat to the left of the typewriter but the finished writing always ended up on the fire...always. She cracked her knuckles, then began to type. She could make heads twitch now that Carl was dead. She could even make the mouths open. Sometimes they screamed but she could handle that because they never opened their eyes unless they screamed first - that was like a rule or something.

Carl's head lay on the desk in front of the typewriter, his mouth slack, his eyes squeezed tight shut. Jennifer lit a cigarette. She leaned back in the chair and tried to look mysterious. It was time to work the magic.

Bare Midriff

S M Vickerman

Midday. The heat a thudding pulse in my organs, every cell throbbing like four hours into a rave, white light searing my sockets. Like a mad dog I'm out in it - foreigners are crazy. But there's no-one with that pitying look: they're all laying dormant indoors. Though there aren't any doors, just black squares suspended in dazzling white. I'm shimmying along the street with a spinning head, high on hormones. My medication, schlucked back before I set out, is a fizzing cocktail.

On my first day, the journey was a wild tango.

It was evening. The sandy track slithered yellow. At that hour the doorways billowed colour. The aim of the dance was to fling you to your destination; up, down. The colours jangled. I was panting, speedy, buzzing like acid nights in Brixton, on the pull in Heaven. But instead of flashing disco lights it was garish people and objects slipping and sliding, kaleidoscopic. Stalls hung with lanterns crushed into each other along the street like a motorway pile-up. I was jiving with a million partners; body-parts engaging, pulling apart like in a dance bar, some pick-up joint. Fabulous. But the sweat was not from dancing, not from shagging afterwards with whoever. The sweat - it was from living. My nostrils widened, snorting a fix of the pungent stench: refuse-piles of steaming vegetation, slicks of coconut oil on black heads smooth as latex. Jasmine in my face, sweet, alluring; wilting in the ropes of hair that tethered the women. Tiny women - like girls.

My first journey to the orphanage.

Stepping out at dusk, heart palpitating. Pricks of light in clay pots in every nook and cranny. A good effect; they could use it in a restaurant somewhere stylish. Islington. I'm hopping about off-balance in all the pushing, and I get a sudden whiff of squelching mango peel. My foot goes through it into a rut, and black water seeps over my sandal, warm gravy between my toes. My toes are splayed, enjoying it. My sari is a cardboard sheet on my back, still rigid with shop starch. The lady in the shop the day before, she had made assumptions, which I can't blame her for. Why does a guy want a sari?

'Wedding?' she asked, and she started pulling out all these fabulous red, gauzy, embroidered hanks of cloth with gold lamé border designs; I mean gorgeous.

'Very fine, very fine', she was going. I couldn't decide, then took a green one.

That first walk.

That indescribably exciting evening when I search out the orphanage the first time, wearing my sari. The underskirt is sticking round my perspiring legs. My sandals are coughing up sand and the rotting litter of the market place and I'm caught up in this tango, being flung from one side to the other. It's exhilarating. And all of a sudden, like a Grimm's fairytale, there's an old woman with one tooth smiling up at me. Spices for sale are arranged in small heaps on a checked cotton rag. I bend forward, low down, and finger the little greasy packets of yellow and red powders. I'm aware of my choli squeezing the flesh of my upper arms, and bagging out at the front. I can just feel the cloth like a vibration on the tips of my nipple-rings. The long board of my sari is swinging forward from my shoulder. The squatting woman reaches up to hold it back. A snake arm, lumpen-veined; an erection in a loose sheath of skin. The sudden shade of the sari is intense, like the thick heat inside a zipped-up tent. We are so close I'm breathing her in. It's like looking each other over in a sauna; that intimate. The pocket of air we're in is dense with aromatic spices and the radiations of our bodies.

A quick movement. She is running her fingers along my chin, grinning. Shit. After I've been feeling so...

She is a gnarled and wrinkled little knot. She cackles, as old women with only one tooth do. She knows. Bright beady eyes peck about on her stall until she locates some cards of tiny glittery stickers in cellophane wrappers. The earth beside her cloth is cracked, caked, like a sunburn blister gone scabby. She says puttu or I don't know what, and hands me one of the flat packets. The photograph on the wrapper shows an Indian movie star. She's got Princess Di hair apart from it being black, and loads of lipstick, and a heart-shaped purple spot in the middle of her forehead to match her sari. The glitter-stickers turn out to be small dots, large dots, and tear-shapes; gold-edged, velvet-finished, or plain; vermillion, black, scarlet, blue. The evening sun is a spot like a tangerine. The old woman sifts out a green tearshape, peels off the back and with tentacle fingers, smoothes it in place between my eyebrows.

An auto-rickshaw is hobbling and honking between the potholes like a shiny black beetle. People are cha cha cha-ing all over the place to get out of the way and I'm partying again in a boogie of colour and noise, the crowd nearly swinging me off my feet. But I twist round as I'm carried away, and I see the old woman's smiling red orifice turned up. One tooth. She hawks and spits next to her cloth. The glistening deposit is the scarlet of betel nut like a blood clot. Her grin is - I mean - wicked.

The crowd is a sponge soaking up flesh. It mops the narrow street from side to side, and I'm compressed in the middle so that liquid seeps out of me and trickles down my back and front; crawling, sluggish, through my thinning-out pubic hair to my scrotum, then racing down my legs like ants. My skin is truly an organ, like they told us at school. I'm feeling the press of anonymous flesh via every molecule. It is saturating my senses and draining off my body fluid in a climatic cycle. Like a sponge I am engorged.

I'm a head taller than the oily, undulating surface of the crowd. Shimmering before me is a former colonial palace that's been brought down. For some reason it's peppermint green. It has white shutters, red roof tiles, everything cracked. The crowd regurgitates me into an empty space by the building's flaking wall. I'm sort of swaying a bit, blinking, as if I've just come out of the Odeon. Ooh... heaven. I'm hyped, tingly; lingeringly excited, the blood of strangers pumping in me like a night on the heath. Only this excitement isn't that. This is from living. It takes a while for my heart to calm down. Now I'm feeling wrung out; spent. But I have arrived, and it's all within my grasp. Awesomely close.

My first entry.

I move into the shade of the entrance. A palm awning that would be stylish on a shop front in Kensington. There's a glorious salmon-pink madonna looking to heaven from a niche. This has to be the place. Evening sunbeams are filtering through the latticework, dappling her skin like an after-glow.

A dim hallway through a blistered door. A scrubbed stone floor. It looks as though it will be cooler, but it isn't. A muzzy stillness blocking out the rickshaw horns, marketeers and chickens like amnesia. My sandals are leaving white footprints in the dark. I slip them off, kick them to the side. The hallway is open at the far end of a dazzling quadrangle. Tranquil but vibrant, like a sannyasi humming in meditation. Cracked earthenware pots of different sizes are clustered in corners, brown brittle shrubs sticking out, dried to a crisp. There might be cobras nestling between them; I'm steering clear. Across the sunbathed square, a cavernous verandah. Draped white mosquito nets, ghostly in the dense shadows. Enormous black crows cawing on the roof. They're watching me. For a moment it's as unreal as a filmset; maybe Hitchcock. A tremor runs through me. It's then that I notice the chanting. A female voice, thin as a needle, scratching out a tuneless rhythm deep inside: Christu, jaya jaya. Christu, jaya jaya. I sit on a little bench just in the shade and tuck the trailing bottom of my sari up, in case of scorpions. I just sit, contemplating my destiny. First day of rest of life, type thing. Everything before, a misguided waste. Now, waiting out my time till the op, I'm on track.

A movement in the blackness of the verandah.

'Oh! You are wearing a sari. Very beautiful!'

My first encounter with Sister Shanti. I am gratified. Affirmed. She is walking across the carpet of evening sunlight, radiant. I feel it. There's a barefoot child in a washed-out, too-short frock attached to the nun's knee, moving as one with her. I am tantalised. As a woman she is slender and elegant, draped in plain dark cloth. As a nun she is serene and perfect, her sari miraculously free of dust. This nun-woman is softly fondling the child's head without looking down. Kohl-pencil rings enlarge the girl's solemn stare. I'm transfixed by the look, the sad little face like my childhood panda, and I hold out my hand, smiling encouragement. There's a stick-on circle of red felt on the child's damp forehead. A million tiny glass bangles tinkle on each skinny forearm. The birds clamour on high above a scene that is bathed in gold like the nativity. I've got the glow of Christmas morning and the overwhelming urge to cuddle this child, smoothe her hair.

That first evening.

I have felt like that ever since. I have also felt my chin smoothe off, my breasts fill out proudly, as the hormones transform, softening me to a peach. These days I tiptoe through the sleeping market street after taking my medication, in the furnace of midday. I avoid the dance with the crowds by travelling from the hostel at that hour. That way I save myself, arriving unspent.

In a spartan interior room, the little ones squall in iron cots. The floor shines black like sea-washed rock, and the windows are of net, not glass. The babies lie on their backs, waving their fists, naked and angry. Or sometimes motionless, like the scene on a fly-paper. I just get on with the job, the heat loud in my ears. Loud, yet intimate, like beating hearts in the crush of a nightclub. I squat like the women do, cradling, rocking. My sweat mingles with the whitewash where I lean, milky stains running down my drapery. Sometimes a tiny hand reaches out to me with longing, touches the white ripple of flesh at my midriff beneath the limp swathe of sari. I get a hit.

Sister Shanti has mistaken me for a saint. She said that I'm fulfilled by my selfless love for others and that I have found my vocation. I must admit I tried the halo on for a moment, wondering. I've had it in my head that I'm the exact opposite of what she thinks. But maybe she's right - maybe I've almost become that... that loving-type person. Self-sacrificing. Maternal. Every day feeding, washing, holding, loving. I walk into the circle and feel my sari touched and pulled by hands which have nothing else to reach for. Their trust is overwhelming. Every day there is a crying need. Here, love is just necessary. My large, white hands enfold each little creature one by one. Turn by turn I nurture them; give them everything. I find it comes - yes - naturally to me. For a time, I save them from their sweating plastic mattresses and the monotony of staring, unseeing, at lizards on the ceiling. For a time, they are satisfied.

As for me, I'm insatiable. Their greediness for my cuddles is my food. When their faces unfurl and become calm, I fill up. When their eyes implore me to hold them for ever I nearly burst. As I'm stuffing yellow rice-food into mouths, using my fingers as a spoon, I'm gorging myself on the sensation of being needed. It's the gluttony of motherhood, and I am in on the secret. I am party to the bingeing that mothers do.

Here, I have already thrown off the apparel of my oppression. Here, in this peppermint green universe with no boundaries, I have penetrated the exclusion zone, and entered the realm of the female. Loving, serving, offering with all my physical capacity, I get a rush. It's the calling of my body and soul. Here, I am at the pinnacle of aliveness. I end each day feeling replete, spilling over with contentment. And when I lie on my bed, I start lusting for the next day because I know now I can have more.

The Serpent

Sitara Khan

Soft flickers of light touch my slothful eyelids with persistent rhythmic strokes, rippling as they caress. The tactile sensation serves only to lengthen my longing for sleep. Now the passing breeze is beckoned to help me waken, brushing against my languid body. As this too proves fruitless, it cradles me into its lap, rocking me from side to side, singing in my ears. The melodious singing changes to a shrill bellowing:

'It's seven o'clock, Salma,' shrieks my brother, Jamal. 'In fact it is now six minutes past seven and Mum said if you don't get out of bed this minute and make our breakfast, she'll be here herself. And you know what that means?'

I do know what that means and I'm not going to argue. My mind's in no mood to engage. Where is the Chinese clock with its chime? The neighbour's car engine roars, a definite reminder that the day has begun. I want a few more moments of snug communion with my night's companion. I try to stretch my arm to reach for the slipper to throw at my brother. He is in luck today for the arm refuses to obey my command. This unannounced strike is out of character. Perhaps it has pins and needles, gone to sleep as they say. I will rub the limp-strike hand with the other to bring it back to life.

No amount of effort produces any movement. My arms are strapped to my back: a punishment for not doing my homework. It's that Mr Smith, wobbling up and down the aisle in our maths class, buttoning his creased polyester cotton shirt over his beer barrel. He always ties my arms behind my back when he's bored with teaching maths or wants to make an example of me for fooling around instead of working. I've become resigned to this little treat - acting as a clown in a circus, mimicking his walk and winning the respect of all my class-fans. He does eventually put me out of my misery, usually when the bell goes. So, I'll have to wait for a while longer. In the mean time, I'll enjoy the power. I often wonder why I have been given a pair of arms just to hang my hands on. The hands with dainty fingers are only there to clean corners and crevices. I often draw them under my armpits to protect them. They are now close to me for ever.

In a few more cosy moments I'll be able to just kick off the duvet and face the world. Just kick it off with my legs and jump out. They aren't much use for anything else in our

Chemical Age of science and automation. We never have to use them to walk and fetch water from the well or coal from the cellar. All our jobs are done sitting down. Everything happens at the flick of a switch. We can do our shopping and anything else we need by speaking to the television screen. That is when it is not being used by the Mind Police.

Mind Police. No. Never: we are an advanced and civilised democracy. We do every thing with fine precision and very skilfully, taking away those parts of the brain which could become problematic to the Public Interest. Once that's done, we rinse the brain clean, so that it is only receptive to the concept of the Mind Police — we are all alluring, enticing through the television screen and other imperial institutions. We start the process to ensure compliance. The education service is one of our keys. And in the Public Interest it's done in the name of achieving high educational standards.

That sounds painful. Besides, I thought that the brain was the master power-house of the body. How can you function without all of its discriminating and critical faculties?

Don't be naive; this is laser surgery. Performed by electrically transmitted neuro- waves in the safety and privacy of your own home or even as you go about your daily business. Simply dissolves the unnecessary molecules whilst you are anaesthetised.

I don't remember ever being anaesthetised. I would never consent to such a thing. I don't believe in chemicals.

That is the beauty of it; no consent or belief is necessary, and it all happens without you even being aware.

Anyway my legs; they always cause me such trouble. It would be much easier to do without legs altogether. We have automated chariots for swishing along on the surface or flying through the atmosphere. I never knew what to do with my legs. They always seemed so undignified just dangling from my body: not quite long enough to reach the floor. This was the one chance for them to come in to their own: kick the duvet off. They have withdrawn their services, it seems. I will get up and see what is happening. Or at least turn my head round. I really must make a move. My head, my head! It feels like lead. I have slept too long. It's always difficult to strike the right balance between having enough sleep and over doing it.

It's bruised from all the slippers you've had on your head.

No, no, they've performed a lobotomy. They've taken my brain out. How am I to think without a brain?

Not necessary.

But how can we compete on the world market? It is all brain-power now. I *need* my brain. That was the best part of me.

You certainly do not need the full capacity you had.

You mean they have taken my brain away whilst I was asleep? Innocently asleep in my own bed.

Don't worry though, you have been supplied with another set of faculties, more appropriate for your needs.

I need my full brain to do my work; to think; to make decisions.

All your worries have been taken care of. All decisions are made for you. Your duties are clearly defined. You are now the Queen.

Me! I am one of the lumpen proletariat, not blue blooded. Anyway, the Queen has a lot of responsibility and all I can offer is an aching, shrunken head. I can't think.

Not necessary. Leave it to The Crown. Programmed accurately for all eventualities.

This is a matter of civil liberties. My brain taken away whilst I was asleep!

You are the Queen now, not a subject. You need to rest from all that nonsense about thinking.

I must say, I am secretly rather tempted by the idea of a true blue Queen, draped in fine robes, sitting upon the Peacock Throne. Deep purple brocade woven with pure gold and white silk thread in rosette bloom, Shanghai design. Or skin tight black jersey with silver lurex in herringbone pattern, and The Crown dazzling with the Kohi-noor diamond.

Shuu... Don't mention that. The Kohi-noor is unlucky and has brought down many a kingdom. Remember Kashmir and the Nizam's Hyder Abad and all the troubles of the Windsor's? It suited the thieving Windsors no more than it did its predecessors. Don't be superstitious. Just enjoy the moment; it may never happen to you.

Yes, people coming to me bowing and scraping, bearing gifts and currying favours as if I were some goddess with supernatural powers to grant their wishes, even if I am... I really must get up to investigate. Hark now! Listen. What is this music which calls my soul? The bansry, the mountain flute. I must dance. I must try despite my old bones. Not so. My spineless fluid body uncoils itself, swaying from side to side, craning the neck to locate the source. The beturbaned green eyed god sits playing just for me. I will dance to his tune. He shall play to my rhythm. He is mine forever.

These emotions are false. They are not natural. My dutiful daughter. My little princess. You evil temptress. You sneaked into his heart then poisoned, condemned the entire race. You committed the original sin. You can't trust men: they're two timers - all of them.

You need love. Without love there is no life.

They're spineless. He'll be on his way and you'll be left with half a dozen children before you've had time to scratch your head.

I will slither and creep up at his feet. SSSSir at your service.

How degrading!

In love and war all is permitted.

There is no love. He is merely after your body. The skin. The slave trade. Not that kind of slavery though. Trust me. Your skin is so precious. The psychedelic accessories.

I will smother him with my kisses and penetrate his deeply set eyes.

You really do get back what you give out. Multiplied. Look at the grotto's stalactites hanging like garlands on shrines. I will make a wish. Penny for your thought.

Secret. Secret.

I must wake up and explore the palace. My palace of millenniums past. Labyrinthine dark passages which lead to dimly lit chambers, infused with shattered hopes, littered with ancient, depthless pools. Offerings of flowers are made to Jupiter or Cupid. I am casting off my old skin; progeny too; and emerging rejuvenated. I was about to consume the lot, but hungrier eyes waited in the wings. The pitiful beings snatched off my poisoned skin to heal. Overcome by momentary compassion, I nearly released my most deadly weapon. But, cautioned by the perennial wise-mind, I have gained composure. I retain my power now, to heal or harm; I am the mistress in charge.

You can't trust her as far as you can throw her. That's if you could ever pick her up, the slimy mess. They can creep up on you unawares, dangling from ceilings, or spring up from under your feet. Danger! Snakes! Keep Clear!

No it's exciting; intriguing. If only she could be seduced by a tantalising trap, all the treasure would be yours. Yes, deeply hidden, almost forgotten: all yours.

Jealously guarding the dowry received, I the baptised nimble Queen, sit at the altar of treasure dreams. Inch by inch my body is wrapped in warm, silken, slithery spirals. My abdomen gripped tightly. Embalmed and mummified, I lie still, my face still moist, smothered in kisses. The tell-tale ears betray intimate, whispered hisses. The clock strikes. I count. Eight o'clock. There is noise outside. Footsteps on the staircase. A doorway thrown open. A voice bellows:

'That's it! I've had enough. Get up now or else…'

Jamal wrenches off the duvet, but movement stops. His

hand suspended in mid air, his eyes widening. Time is frozen. He drops the duvet. He runs out of the room. Reverberating from wall to wall in my new chasm are his horrified screams of:

'Mother! Serpent! Serpent! Serpent!'

Elsewhere

Sue Wood

On the day of the fair, the cows showed us that it was going to rain. Their heads drooped and dreamed into buttercups, with legs tucked under them like those docile cream-jug creatures that once grazed the safe shelves of Mam's cool larder...

Quite unlike the stinking, fly-blown heap I once remembered finding beside the road into Winton, a dark thread of blood crusted around the little hole in its head. Its belly growing rounder and rounder in the August heat, and the stained grass and smell staying for weeks after it had been dragged away. Our old, grass-sweet Cherry, a mess of putrefaction and flies. Abraham and I had run past the spot every day, to and from school, until we forgot why we always ran, just there.

Abe was not a real brother because Ma had come across him as sort of stray. Like the twin lambs, he was too much for his real mother and we took him in. Often he seemed too much for us. I was five years old when he came and at the age when I cheered to the thought of a brother to come round the farm with me. I still remember my disappointment when Mam brought him in. I had set up an intricate walkway of planks on creosote barrels in the yard, knowing that being able to navigate from plank to plank, at a brisk trot, was sure to impress my new brother. I would guide him round. That way I figured I would be in charge, and he would know his place in the yard, the lane to the hummocks' field, the cubby-hole under the hens' house and Mam's warm, yeasty kitchen.

Mam had been away for a whole night, to fetch him over. And Aunt Maudie forgot to give me an egg with a knitted woolly hat on its head. I had been given two for Christmas, one for me and one for luck. My brother Abe was to have the second one. I had determined on that. I heard Finney barking outside and Mam came in with a parcel of white laundry. I thought she was about to open the copper-lid when I noticed a fist clenching out of the parcel. Then a thin wail and then two legs kicking like the porkers do, just after Daddy Greensop has gone right across the baby-skin under their chins with his killing knife. Mam looked pleased, the sort of pleased she looked when she had won a china bowl at Bartle Fair, or Dad had sold all the fat lambs.

'I've got a brother for you, Rosie', Mam said. I stood beside the dresser and waited. The laundry milled up and down in Mam's arms, and my new brother Abe shrieked.

Mam uncovered his face, a spasm of keening flesh pulsed around the pit of his mouth, a little hole through which Abe drilled his appalling indignation. I put my hands to my ears and ran into the yard. The barrels and planks spread out like a crazy sheep-pen and I ran round and round inside the chest-high barriers, hearing not the comfortable clucking of the hens, but the wild noises of the ewes calling and calling the baby-names of their lambs when Dad had the lambs trucked up and ready. And inside the metal box of the truck, the lambs shrieked and soiled themselves. Some would be allowed to grow a bit, elsewhere. That's what Mam said, but I did not like the feel of elsewhere. Neither did my brother Abe. I shoved the planks off the barrels and, surrounded by angles of rough wood and the great clanging bellies of the barrels, for the first of many times, I sat and wept for my brother Abe.

So the day of the fair had not started out rainy. Abe, who was now nearly eleven, was up early as usual, sloping round the empty house in that padding soft way that made him come upon you unexpected, like meeting a sauntering fox the other side of an oak-thicket. People jumped or froze when they came across Abe. He followed his own line of scent and often seemed as startled as others when they got into his patch. Sometimes he stood listening, his red-gold hair stirring, his green and gold eyes focused away beyond the kitchen's jumble of milk jugs, Mam's preserves and the skittering of Trinket's newest kittens. Dad had long stopped saying 'A penny for them.' Abe would have cost too many pennies. Instead Dad would work round Abe, not brushing into him, but shaking his head in a worried way. Dad loved noise and people and laughter: he touched our hands, made even Aunt Maudie dance at Christmas so that she remembered how young legs felt, because hers creaked so. But Dad never got Abe to dance. He did not understand such things and could not join in Christmas games or Harvest Home in the big barn.

'Coming to Rystone Common today?' I asked. 'There's Billings Circus and some rides'. Above all I wanted to wear my new Liberty cotton dress. Mam said it looked like the corn-fields in her day. All sprinkles of flowers and heaving wheat, she said with a sly twinkle. I think the wheat was a reference to my own swelling breasts, which I alternately obscured under big, yoked blouses or presented shyly to public gaze in a tight bodice that thrust everything upwards, and dangerously outwards. I was ready for just a touch of adventure in the meadow of my Liberty dress.

So it was that we set off across the fields, with a puckering of clouds just beyond Ditchley Hill and the cows were already kneeling-up in the grass, half-way between rain and sun. Abe sloped ahead. Poked with a stick in holes and field-corners as if it had been a long nuzzling nose, turning up whole histories of shrews and rabbits and badgers. He used his nose more than his eyes to sense up people. Abe could figure out whether the pot-mender man had got the hens' eggs with a sniff of his nose. Counting things, school sums or eggs, made him puzzled. He got there quicker otherways. Sometimes he would snap at those big, fat horse-flies, his thin, reddish hands scissoring like jaws. And sometimes he would listen, his green-gold eyes searching somewhere that was not the farm. I often wondered if it was another kind of elsewhere that he looked and listened out for.

Abe didn't speak much, but that was because he knew about things before you'd got round to fitting the words. He spat words out like pig-gristle and they came out all wrong. Mam said he had a defect. Like Patty's calf being born with its tongue all grown out to the size of a Christmas ox-tongue. It had stood next to Patty with its mouth wedged open. Great globs of spit stuck on its legs, unable to suck. But my brother Abe had a red, sharp, little tongue. His defect was inside.

As we rounded the hill, I could hear the merry-go-rounds and the shunt, shunt of the great steam engines. Coal and engine oil, toffee, onions, beer, a faint tang of wild beasts and urine made Abe stand still, his back quivering slightly. He grinned. His nose sorted the scents. Then we streaked across the bumpy sheep-pasture, over a rattling wooden bridge and into the thick mass of people.

A group of boys watched us as we ran up to the Skelter. They were from the High School and knew Abe because he had been in the Infants School for years. He helped Miss Blinson with sand and paints for the little ones and gave out the bottles of milk as if each child had won a special prize, everyday. Abe did not like the big boys. He would squeeze under a laurel bush in the caretaker's yard, curled up small, panting and shaking until they passed the gates. 'Lubber lips! Pig-hole! Fox stink!' They smirked and showed their teeth at us. I grabbed Abe's arm and we headed for the merry-go-round. Abe loved sitting up high and looking down. Spinning together, his small red arm round the floating poppies and wheat sprigs of my Liberty dress and the fair-ground streaming away from us with its bobbing clots of faces, we could have been going somewhere else.

The ride stopped and we sidled through the crowd. Big spots of warm summer rain began to fall and Abe crouched down into his shoulders, his belly lower to the ground, trying to slip away.

Just the snap of a twig and the dark shadow in the hen-house has gone.

We made for the line of booths and tents at the edge of the field. Tired-looking men in clothes like the pedlar-man's stood in front of screened-off dingy bolt-holes. This was where they kept the freak shows. I'd once seen a calf with two heads that called and called for its mother. The mouths did not bellow together. I am glad our calf died. Somehow the bearded lady always looked like old Mummy Greensop, only younger and sad. But today there was a new show 'The Vixen Woman and her Cubs'. Abe and I paid the entry fees and, ducking under a dirty piece of sheeting, went inside.

A dull red light lit up the far corner of the tent. As we went over towards it we saw a big heap of straw. Under the straw there were quiet movements and little nuzzling squeaks and slurps. Abe stood and slowly the thick red hair on his neck and head stirred and stood up with a little shivering ripple. His nostrils opened into dark searching holes and a strange rumbling growl, low and insistent, came up from his throat. I tried to grab Abe and take him away. But as I turned a man's voice came from one side 'Gerrup you flinking red slut! You've got some gawkers. Show yer feathers now!'

The straw rustled, parted, and a woman's figure slowly stood up before us. She was thin and tall and covered from head to foot in fine bristly red hair. Her face was horribly stretched out round the nose into a matted, hairy muzzle and on her bare rump was a bedraggled fox's brush. From her swinging teat hung a protesting fox cub, its paws trailing against her thin stomach. She grinned in our direction and hoisting up the cub into her arm-pit, turned and stuck out her rump with its glued on tail. A hot rank stink made me feel sick. I wanted air.

Then Abe sprang. I saw his teeth glint as he hurled himself towards her shaggy back-side. His red, bristly arm came down on her neck and there was a snapping noise.

Twigs breaking, the quick bite to the throat and the hen-house silent and bloodied.

My brother Abe was taken away. I do not know where he went or if that elsewhere is a better one for him. Each Spring I stuff the pillow over my ears when the ewes cry out for their lambs.

Thomas

Ian Cusack

Noise always disturbed Karen. Whether she was sleeping, reading or working, any external volume would distract and disrupt her. She didn't get scared, she got annoyed. Outside was hostile. It took her ten minutes to lower herself off the sofa-bed, crawl across the basement and then climb the step ladders. Her dogs, Rex and Peter, were barking outside. Normally they hunted berries in the wood, which Karen turned into a rich jam, for mail order sale. The dogs howled then gaped, revealing the craters in their gums that had once held teeth, but now were berry stores. At their feet lay a smaller crop than usual; behind them knelt Karen's daughter, Vicky. She was holding an infant boy in her arms.

Seeing Vicky made Karen angry at her daughter's indolence. The dogs should have been collecting berries until their mouth-stores were full. On a normal day they would hunt until two, return, then spit the fruit into a galvanised zinc funnel that fed the berries down a plastic tube and into an earthenware bowl, half filled with cold water. After soaking them for an hour, Karen would pulp the flesh, then begin boiling it with sugar to make the jam. Today there was not enough fruit to make a batch and she felt annoyed by this. However, Vicky's strange stance shifted Karen's attention to her daughter. Vicky was not normally a cause of interest to her mother, nor to anyone really.

Karen grabbed the plastic berry-tube out of the bowl and called through it. The zinc funnel acted as a partially successful megaphone, amplifying the volume of Karen's message, but failing to catch the sense of irritation in her voice.

'What the hell are you doing? Down here, now. How am I supposed to make a living with only half the usual amount of berries? And where did you get that bloody kid from?'

As Vicky stood up she allowed the small boy to drop and land head first on the lawn. Karen balked at this. Before she could react, Vicky scooped up the child and came into the basement that had once been a store for fuel, but now represented the living and working space for 95% of Karen's life. She always felt irritated in the presence of her daughter. She preferred the dogs, even though they were strictly for work, and not pets; no affection could be lavished on them. Hence they remained lying on the grass beside the leaf-choked carp pond, cleaning their genitals with callused tongues.

'I'm sorry Mum, but it was cold out today and the dogs were getting all whiney so I started to come back a bit early. We could still have got a three quarter crop, but once we found this, I had to come home right quickly.'

This was what Karen had taken for a small child. It was not in fact an infant, but an eerily accurate sculpture of a baby boy, the hollow torso fashioned out of wood with a padded silken face, arms and legs. The hair was human rather than an inflexible nylon weave, and the mouth consisted of hard plastic teeth, but not perfect ones; some were missing, others overlapped and crossed, with chips and yellow discolourations of tartar. The tongue was of pliable rubber and the mouth and tonsils were a light polymer that gave without ripping. The eyes were sealed. Close inspection revealed a kind of anatomical attention to detail that unnerved as well as fascinated. The doll was dressed in a plain blue tee shirt and shorts set, with *Bugs Bunny* embossed trainers and socks.

Perhaps the strangest thing was how it pissed. Having undressed the doll, looking for a return address or something to indicate its origin, Karen and Vicky noticed the tiny but anatomically accurate, penis and empty scrotum sac. The legs detached, revealing a thin copper pipe that led from a reservoir in the throat through the body to the penis. The tube, intricately kinked and bent, was protected by a perspex sleeve built around it to stop movement and general wear and tear which might cause the pipe to snap. Vicky put a bottle to the back of its mouth and the doll swallowed quarter of a pint of liquid, which remained in the reservoir until it worked its way down to the penis. No sucking was possible as the doll was not mechanised. The point of the bends and kinks in the tube, they realised, was to stop the doll urinating straight after drinking; instead the diversions and blind alleys made it take ten minutes or so to begin pissing. The choice of copper for the piping became obvious. Aged copper adopts a greenish hue that coloured the pure water Vicky had given the doll. Karen thought about feeding it tomato juice, just to see her daughter's reaction. They experimented and discovered that it was possible for the doll to piss with or without legs, sitting or standing, although the flow lessened for gravitational reasons when the doll was sitting.

They dressed the doll again and sat it upright on the window ledge, looking out at ankle level to the lawn, then they drank coffee. Karen was quieter now, Vicky relieved that the intervention of the doll had avoided the certainty of a row. Karen drained her cup then turned to her daughter.

'I suppose finding something like that out in the woods would have put the wind up you a bit, looking so much like a dead baby and that, but I can't understand why you had to come tearing back here.'

Vicky blanched visibly, then sighed with pathetic honesty.

'I wasn't frightened, Mum. I just loved him at first sight. I've decided to call him Thomas.'

Karen wrinkled her nose in disgust both at the sentiment her daughter had just expressed, and at the smell coming from the doll; a sort of mushroomy, rotting leaves odour. Vicky supposed that Thomas, as she insisted on calling it, had been in the woods for at least a few days. She cured the stench by washing and tumble drying his clothes. Karen was not pleased by Vicky's maternal instincts. The most sickening thing was seeing her own daughter tenderly wrap the thing in a small blanket while the clothes were in the wash, supposedly to stop him feeling the cold. It was at this point Karen vowed she would destroy the doll. Of course it would have been easy to just grab the thing and fling it on the fire, or smash it to pieces with her hammer, but the indecent display of second rate mother-love her daughter was showing to this toy needed to be cured properly. Karen reasoned it would be in Vicky's best interests to realise now that men and children were not worthy of affection; perhaps it was even time to show Vicky that her mother viewed her as a servant and not a loved one. The only creatures that Karen didn't despise couldn't speak, couldn't look after themselves without her, and did everything they were told: her dogs.

Vicky's obsession with cleaning Thomas took several hours which Karen felt could have been spent more profitably collecting berries. The poor haul of fruit from the day before would rot if she did not use it soon. By the time Vicky had finished messing with Thomas, dressing him and pouring lime cordial down his gullet to make the piss seem realistic, it was late afternoon. Karen had grown steadily more irritated by the bored Alsatians under her feet. Allowing them out in the garden had been only partially successful. Admittedly she could get on with the jam, but the swollen bladders and distended bowels of the two dogs had been voided on her lawn, already awash with fallen leaves. When Vicky came down into the cellar, proudly brandishing the doll in front of her, Karen was beyond tolerating her daughter's whims any longer.

'For Christ sake, get that stupid toy away from me! You're seventeen you know, not seven. I needed more berries today. This lot won't make a full load. Get down in the garden and pick me some apples so I can at least make some mixed preserve. And when you've done that, clear the lawn.'

It seemed as if Vicky might cry; her eyes shone and she bit her lip. Cuddling Thomas tightly, she went back upstairs, apparently to get her shoes, but really to put Thomas down for his afternoon sleep.

Five minutes later Vicky was outside, halfway up a pair of stepladders. She was collecting the miniature orange pippins that had not been pecked at by birds, placing them in a white canvas bag, stained by juice and earth. The dogs circled the ladders, barking excitedly. She descended and emptied the bag into a wicker basket, then busied herself with dividing the windfalls into the edible for the preserve, and the rotten, which the dogs carried three at a time to the compost heap. The good apples would be crushed and blended with the pulped berries and several pounds of sugar, then the mixture set to boil. Reduced to a simmer, the cooking would take several hours.

When Vicky had collected all the apples, Karen sent her out into the woods with the dogs, not to collect berries, but for exercise. On hearing the faint clang of the garden gate, Karen opened a window to let out steam. She caught the fragrance of her daughter's sly cigarette on the breeze and set her face with a harder aspect than even Vicky was used to. She knew her daughter would be gone for hours. Karen rooted out a pair of pliers and the wire clippers from her tool-box, then with a grim smile began to ascend the staircase. She fancied that she could hear a small child crying up there.

Seeing the Light

Sue Wilsea

She had a son called Ben who was her third child and he, who had been a massive unbabylike blob when born, cried day and night, night and day. He was a stain - ugly, rust coloured - which seeped through the thin protective membrane of her ownness; an immovable stain. She cherished him the way you cherish an imperfection, a blemish on the otherwise smooth skin of her life. Ben developed into the child no-one wanted around, the child with whom other parents favourably compared their own. He destroyed possessions, both his own and others, and underwent mood swings that were sudden and violent. He hated with venom but became passionately absorbed in people and things too. The greatest miracle, as far as she was concerned, was that she went on loving him despite it all, defending the indefensible, unintentionally spinning a cocoon of care and concern around the two of them that excluded others.

One scorching summer's day, when Ben was about five, the two of them stood outside the house waiting for the rest of the family to leave for a day out in Scarborough. For what seemed like hours a welter of buckets, spades, towels, beachballs, deckchairs and holdalls had mounted in the hallway. The carpet became gritty underfoot from last year's sand. The dank, fishy smell of seaweed hung on the air. Ben had refused to go. He hated the noise of the seaside, was frightened of seagulls, donkeys, amusement arcades and waves, and she had said she might as well stay with him. Her husband shrugged, the other two pulled faces and returned to their dispute about the relative merits of North or South Bay. Yet Ben resented them going and melded his body into her side, whimpering like a small animal as she made sandwiches and divided them into three neat parcels. Eventually, the car was loaded. Squinting her eyes against the angry sun, it seemed to swell in front of her until it became one large, metallic carapace oozing sweat and the smell of plastic. The children pushed their faces up against the glass, distorting and flattening them in order to frighten Ben. She scolded, soothed and exchanged essential information and a dry brush of the lips with her husband. Finally he backed slowly down the drive. Leaning out of the windows and banging the sides of the car, the children screeched with excitement while Ben blocked his ears against the horrible noise. As the dust settled back on the driveway, the two of them stood in silence feeling the beat of the sun on their heads. In the distance she could hear a lawnmower, the creak of a swing, a radio.

Ben wanted to make a lantern. He'd seen one made on a children's television programme and wanted to copy it. She felt the familiar knotting feeling in her belly. Memories of other failed projects were scorched in her mind - the lopsided Christmas fairy they'd made, resulting in him pulling the tree down; their chocolate cake that had hit the kitchen wall like some slapstick pantomime scene. The shouts, tears, mess, recriminations. She started to suggest other alternative activities but one glance at his closed down face and she knew it was useless. Anyway, it was too hot to argue.

They'd gone down to the shed at the bottom of the orchard and found some withies she had once got for a basket making class that she'd quickly had to abandon when Ben refused to go to bed without her there in the house. They soaked the withies in the old rainwater barrel to make them supple, then bent them into petal shapes and bound them with gaffer tape. Ben wanted paper on them; thin paper. Ben wanted thin paper. Impatiently rooting around in the cool darkness of the box room she'd found, inside an otherwise empty shirt box, large sheets of pale pink tissue paper. Sitting back on her heels and holding up to the light one of the gauzy sheets she saw again her pink smudged wedding day; in an orchard bulging with apple blossom rows of trestle tables covered with crisp white damask cloths, these overlaid with sheets of pink tissue; fine Georgian silver, pink roses in silver bowls, soft pink cones of serviettes. There had been so much left over - food, drink, presents, the paper. She drew the paper towards her and smoothed the sheet back over her face so that her lips and nose splayed in a grotesque salmon coloured mask. A shout brought her back to the present. Grabbing the rest of the paper she hurried back outside.

Painstakingly they stretched the paper between the frames until taut. From time to time it would get a crease or would tear slightly from being pulled too tightly. By mutual consent it was scrunched up, an abandoned rose, and another oval of paper carefully cut out. They sat in the long grass totally absorbed in what they were doing. There were wasps after fallen overripe fruit but the two of them were immune. They both wore floppy white hats and their faces, arms and knees became daubed with the white sticky paste they were using. Lunch and tea were snacks brought outside on trays and he, normally so greedy with his food, had barely touched any of it. After lunch he had fallen asleep for an hour or so, and she moved him into the shade where the light dappled his smooth skin, stained with paste, grass and food.

At the end of the afternoon they'd made enough petals and could fasten them together, three layers of them, the different sizes inverted to form a huge fairylike scallop. A candle in a jar and a long pole for holding and carrying completed the creation. She told Ben they would light it when it was dark to get the full effect of the lantern's beauty. He would have his supper and bath and then she would light it. But he wanted the light now. No, later. Why? Because it'll be better then. Why? Because it will be darker. I want it now. Later. Now. Later.

She left him kicking and screaming while she went inside to fetch him a glass of juice. Often tantrums were eased by administering food or drink. She poured Ribena out, taking pleasure in the viscous purple liquid sliding down the side of the glass. The pipes groaned as she turned on the tap in the kitchen and she thought of where she would display the lantern for the others when they returned. She would hang it in the porch, turn off all the downstairs lights and they would see it illuminated as they came up the drive, a beacon of her achievement. She imagined how she would casually describe to her husband the time she and Ben had spent on its construction; how he would have to be impressed by his youngest son's creativity and patience; how she and him could for once unite in parental admiration. Once Ben was settled, perhaps they could have a meal, just the two of them, with candles, wine and soft lights. And afterwards, perhaps they might make love. A thin runnel of sweat trickled between her breasts and she pressed her groin once, twice, against the cold, hard edge of the sink. With a spasm from the tap, water gushed over the top of the glass. Smiling, she poured a little out and went back into the garden.

He had raped it. Every petal had been punched in. Shreds of tissue paper hung limply in surrender from the frame which stood balanced awkwardly on one side like the skeleton of a massacred animal. The jamjar was smashed, the pole snapped in two. He'd even wrenched some of the withies apart, though, lying on the ground, they still clung to their curves as if ashamed of their violation. He stood by the debris, half defiant and half afraid. He was panting, his cheeks were flushed and there was a dark stain on the front of his shorts.

'Mu...m.' A cry of despair, of fear.

'It doesn't matter.'

Then, defeated, she slumped down and cried. The crying took a long time but then again it had waited a long time. It was not just for the broken lantern that she sobbed, but for her broken dreams, for the futility of it all, the exhausting struggle to keep everything together, everything taut.

She remembered the pleading look on his face after he'd done it, while she still lay there in a tangle of skewed clothes and sticky dampness. How she'd felt, bizarrely, a need to protect him, to bend around him like the pliant withies and corral his anger.

'I'm so sorry mum....'

'It doesn't matter.'

'Can we still...? Will it...?'

'Of course we can, love....'

A fairytale wedding, a pink and white confection of hope, followed by ten years and three children. More than many others had. And yet. She shifted position. An apple had leaked its brown mushy ripeness onto her skirt. Ben had moved a little distance away and had squatted down with his back turned.

Later, he had sat on the side of the bed with his back to her, leaning forwards with his head in his hands and she'd run her hand down his spine, cooing 'It doesn't matter, love... it doesn't matter...'

The air turned cool, the leaves started whispering and the ground breathed up its evening moistness. The two of them were still there when the others returned later in the evening to find the house in darkness, no meal cooked and no willing arms for wet clothes, towels and remains of the picnic. Her husband was irritated, expecting praise for what he perceived as his Herculean efforts, and he disappeared inside, pointedly snapping on lights everywhere. The two older children stepped on the detritus of cane, tape and paper as they excitedly told of the castle, the cliff cable car, the lighthouse. They proffered their tacky spoils of sticky rock and lollies, and the present they'd bought for their awkward brother.

He'd just wanted to see the light, Ben told her later, as she tucked the white sheets round his rigid little body and kissed him goodnight. She wouldn't let him see the light and he'd wanted to see it. He'd wanted to see the light. Then, not later. She hadn't let him see the light. His dark, troubled eyes met hers for the merest flicker of time, then he heaved onto his side, hurtfully away from her. She reached for the switch of the bedside lamp and, in that moment before darkness swallowed them both, she saw he clutched tightly in one hand his present from the seaside. Cruel, malicious, or unintentional, she could not tell. Ben's hand gripped a baby's dummy; a giant dummy, moulded in lurid red sugar.

Shop Window

Mandy MacFarlane

Brian started his life in a shop window. He and his fellow babies were arranged in the glass front to show off their best features to the passing public who peered through the glass, intrigued at some of the antics and gestures of the tots, deciding whether or not to buy.

Brian felt isolated. He found it difficult to make contact with his fellows as each one was competing against the other to get bought. They smiled their brightest toothless smiles, gooed and gaaed as hard as they could to make an impression on the browsers and stand out in the crowd.

The babies were looked after by some shopkeepers who lined them up every morning and every evening for a bottle. Occasionally the kids would get an extra suck on a bottle or the odd cuddle, but it was very rare. The shopkeepers were too busy with their accounts to pay attention to a hundred squealing babies, some of whom were severely depressed and sat dead pan when the rush hour brought in a dozen or so shoppers at a time.

Sometimes the shoppers were eager to purchase at first, then disappointment marked their faces when they saw what was on offer. The babies spotted the signs right away, but tried to pretend for their own self-respect that they hadn't noticed. The shopkeeper would reassure the customers, 'Come back next week and have a look then. There's bound to be a new set of deliveries.'

Brian dreamed of the day he could sleep in his own cot and have a family to take care of him rather than an untrained shop assistant just out of school without a clue.

One sultry summer evening Margi, a local woman, had gone shopping down the High Street in search of a hat and had gone in there by mistake, only noticing something was amiss when the usual sign for a six month guarantee plus interest free credit wasn't visible.

Brian remembers sitting in his pram in a bright yellow romper when he spotted Margi and gave her a wave. He tried getting her attention by smiling but as she didn't have her glasses on she didn't notice. Fortunately however, Brian managed to grab hold of her sleeve as she passed. Although bewildered at first by what was on offer, she fell in love with the little bundle and chatted to him for a good half hour before she had to get back to work. Brian had a lump in his throat when she left. He wished every night for her to come back and rescue him.

Luckily, Margi did go back there a few days later with her glasses to pick Brian up and take him home. He was over the moon that she hadn't forgotten him and even happier with his new set of rompers and the collection of antique china dolls that were hanging around Margi's flat.

He was very happy for several months with Margi before he realised that her husband, The Barber, had a serious problem with alcohol and wasn't at all interested in the new addition to their household. When Margi went to work in the evening at the hotel, The Hairdresser hot tailed it down the boozer and left Brian screaming blue murder, on his own, watching telly with a bag of cheese and onion.

Sad to say it didn't end there. Margi didn't appear to have a clue about what was going on and so for many nights Brian stood in his nappies staring out of the window watching The Hairdresser head off down the pub.

This went on for two years. Brian learned very quickly to fend for himself. He found out how to make ham bone soup, mince and tatties and his old favourite, custard and jelly.

By the time Brian was three he was a relatively good cook and had started doing the housework. He cooked breakfast when Margi was on earlies. Bacon, eggs, tomatoes and potato scones were his speciality. Sometimes he'd invite the twins from upstairs, whose mother had run off to California to be a surfer, and their father Donald couldn't boil an egg to save himself, so as means of compensation, took the boys to the chip shop every night. But however many chips the twins ate, they grew thin as rakes. The doctor was called in but even after a thorough examination said he could find nothing wrong. Days passed and the boys got thinner until Donald took them to see Brian for one of his slap up breakfasts. At last their bellies grew larger and the roses appeared back on their cheeks. In exchange the twins, who were a year or so older than Brian, promised to teach him how to read so that he could try out some more complicated recipes. They brought down their school books and began with the alphabet.

One evening Brian found some old scholls that Margi's dad had made her from beechwood, and he tripped along to the hotel to see his mum and get a roast beef sandwich for his tea. He took the opportunity to impress upon Margi the importance of having a well stocked kitchen with decent utensils and several chopping boards. Margi took him up on his suggestion and bought a few things at wholesale prices from the chef.

At five, Brian didn't bother going to school. He decided to give it a miss as he could learn more in his kitchen than a stuffy classroom. The school inspectors dropped in unexpectedly a little while after his fifth birthday, but they were so bowled over by his fruit scones and homemade raspberry jam that they soon forgot why they had come and left incredibly happier than when they'd arrived.

Unfortunately for Brian and Margi, The Hairdresser was still hanging around and tearing off to the pub at the least opportunity. He'd lost his clientele through bad faith and had started stealing money. Some of his oldest customers came round to the house with hair down to their shoulders desperate for him to cut their hair, but no one had lain eyes on The Barber for some time. Brian was greatly relieved and was able to focus totally on his cooking and perfect his recipes. Then just as he and Margi were beginning to relax and feel comfortable again, he would come back sniffing around the place, with one eye on the cooking sherry and the other on the brandy butter. Margi was no help at all to Brian. Whenever The Barber came back she pretended he hadn't, convinced that if she believed he didn't exist, she wouldn't have to face up to the fact that she had made an appalling choice in husbands. Margi left Brian no option but to deal with everything himself. He began to wonder who had rescued who, and if he felt more stress now than he had done when in the shop window. The Barber popped back at odd intervals, never announcing his arrival. Then he would send Brian out to the shop for cigarettes, and when Brian returned, the armagnac for his sweet orange tarts would have vanished.

Brian grew exasperated but found it difficult to say no to The Barber, who was extremely cultivated in the worldly ways of manipulation and cunning. This endless task making tired Brian out. His mood changed and he started moping around uncomfortably while The Barber dried out and slept. He cheered up no end when The Barber went back out on a bender and disappeared for several days at a time. Then Brian's flair returned. His dumplings no longer sagged and his soufflés were once again firm. But this peace would never last long. Back would come The Barber and Brian's anxiety returned, making his custard runny and his jellies unpalatable. He forgot to put the ham bone in his soup and put squid in his seafood cocktail instead of prawns. Brian approached breaking point and was running out of patience. He needed to think of a way to get The Barber out of their lives for good.

One afternoon when The Barber was taking a nap, Brian found some tulip bulbs Margi had hidden in the cellar. He fried them gently, added some stock and croutons he made from stale bread, then served it all up as French onion soup. The Barber lapped it all up then went out on a binge. He never came back to bother either of them again.

In the spring, when she went to plant her tulip bulbs, Margi was faintly bemused that they had disappeared, and that only a few flakes of skin remained.

'Seen my bulbs anywhere, Brian?' she asked in her friendly tone. But he only shook his head and turned his attention to the pastry he was rolling for his steak and kidney pie.

'Hey, why don't we ask the twins and Donald down for dinner?' was Brian's response. He was anxious to divert the conversation. Margi, who was the queen of keeping her head in the sand, knew better than to ever mention the bulb subject again.

Vitezstvi

Daithidh MacEochaidh

So we had won. At last, one final victory, but it could not feel that way. We were on our way home; this our triumph. At first we had no way of telling or deciding in what direction home lay. At times we allowed ourselves to be guided by the rising and the setting of the sun, though we counted time by the moon and even, on occasions, choosing some lone bright star as a signpost. We were lost.

We were the lost, but we were never alone. The whole continent, major and minor, was on the move; mainly ragged bands travelling on foot, but occasionally you would encounter the fortunate few, the lucky ones, whipping or dragging some half-starved horse, mule or donkey; the beast's back bowed by the weight of possessions or children or wives. One horse, one weak dapple grey fell under the burden of salvaged loot and its owner, dead-eyed, whipped and kicked that horse, whipping and kicking long after it had ceased to breathe. We passed on. We had seen worse. Always we had seen worse.

Yet crossroads could still cause problems. Mentally fumbling over which direction to take we were plagued by girls from seven to seventeen, sometimes boys too, who would allow us to do anything we wanted to do for food, for drugs or for some mythic passport that would open up some other world. They could grant us anything but directions home. At crossroads decisions had to be made and we learned to loathe such places.

Once we arrived by chance at the edge of the sea. We washed, we bathed in the cold salt water, its chill soaking deep to the bones, but it did no good. Drying in the sun we still stank of shell-shock sweat and too much war. And my burden, my lone possession, he was already rotten. He was gone, but the sickly sweet smell of carrion could no longer disgust me. I shouldered him, my brother, and we walked the shoreline. For many days we walked. The moon above waxed and waned and we just walked, moving on, always moving on. Every daybreak we would promise ourselves that over the next brow, the next long sweep of headland, we would find the path home.

But this optimism too died. We realised one long night when the moon turned full and the waves licked quick and fast along the seashore that we were not and had never been sea-people. We were in-landers. This sudden sense of belonging, coming after so many years astray, sent our senses reeling. By a rock-pool we wept quite openly, our bodies slumped against one another, my brother and I. Yet at last, a long sorry last, we were going to be on our way home. Home, I whispered in the cold shell of his one good ear. I kissed his brow for joy or for something that just might have been such elation. Shouldering my burden again we picked our way across the pebbled shore, the chuckies clacking like old bones, as we staggered up the raised beach. We fought a way over the rise of the headland, turning our back on the sea, heading, all the time heading home.

And once there was a rumbling, some months after we had found a half-buried road. This rumbling echoing nearer became for us an intimation of something else, something more familiar though we had forgotten precisely what was this other thing. Dodging potholes and ruts and broken tarmac a van drove towards us. There was a young man inside. He was smoking. He was clean-shaven and businesslike.

We had no longer anything left to sell. Neither had we anything simply to barter. We wished the young man luck. He thought us crazy. He told us that we would never make it. He almost begged for us to turn back with him. He was right. But, it no longer mattered.

He made one last offer. His eyes swept over my brother, judging and businesslike. We shook our heads and he u-turned and returned along the broken road. Dead or alive we were no longer for sale. We had a home to find somewhere ahead, always somewhere further to go. There was no longer anything else left for us, but this return to our own homeland.

Besides we had seen what they had done to the dead. The dead were not granted peace; such notions lay in the past. We had been through all that. We were no longer for sale and all that was left to us was to find a way back. This became our mantra. There would be no more breaking of faith. Till my dying breath I pledged my brother that a home, some distant place of rest would be found for us. It was then that the van driver took pity on us, made another last offer that he would drive us at least part of the way home. We shook our heads on hearing this. At last we had learned not to trust, to distrust instinctively. It was time to pick up our bundle and find our own way once more. I draped my brother over my shoulders, tottered, faltered a little, till I found my feet and we moved forward, slowly, paying no heed to the sound of the antiquated van, retreating, on its way to bargain with the horizon.

One day we met an old man in a badly plaited grass-skirt, trying to grow potatoes in the verge of some crumbling highway. At first we did not believe that the ancient would speak to us. But he ambled over, a home-made hoe clutched in his one good hand. He came to us, requiring news, wanting to know if at last it was all over. We made the usual phatic gestures, but the man was not convinced. But we knew it was all finished. We were our own proof. We left the man, grubbing the black earth, safe with his doubts.

Some survive. Some always survive is the hope that keeps everything churning. The ancient would be all right. Some always are. As for us, there was nothing but the long walk despite our failing strength.

At a crossroads, by a broken motel, we lay down and wept. We just wept. For a moment we had lost it. The will, the desire, the wish even, to go on had deserted us. There we would have stayed if an ageing grandmother and grandchild had not chanced our way. Perhaps, we had fallen asleep, for I do not remember their arriving. Suddenly, there was this lady rifling through our clothes and holding on to her shawl a semi-naked girl with empty sockets for eyes.

'What 'live 'un', muttered the lady, spitting into the dust. I warned the lady to leave my brother alone, which she did, though she continued to eye him wistfully.

'He is dead, is he not?' the lady said, more statement than question.

I drew a rusting gun from my jacket and ordered the lady to back off. If they had touched my brother again I would have shot them both, there and then. It would not have been a hard thing to do, not after all this time. Medals, special commissions and bonuses had depended on much worse.

'He is dead, why not give him to us?' pleaded the lady.

But I told her straight, that we were going home. There was a pause then. Her empty gums chewing on several unpleasant thoughts. Then she crept up, crouched low over me. She still wanted the dead.

'Sell me the eyes', she said in a voice hardly above a whisper.

I just shook my head, keeping my gaze fixed on the horizon.

'Go on, just the eyes and you can do 'er, do what you want, as many times you want', the lady offered. Turning to her granddaughter, she said something harsh in some tonal tongue. The girl raised her torn print dress. She was bare, a wretched stretch of flesh. She had been done, done too many times and far too young. But we were going home, my brother and I, a grandmother and a girl with emptied eyes could no longer disturb our nights, hinder our progress. Once some things are done, their hold is forever gone.

I shouldered my brother. I staggered. I found my feet again and turning right I knew perhaps at last where to find our home.

'Bastard, what sort of bastard refuses eyesight to the blind! Can't you see what they have done to my grandchild! Give me his eyes!' the old woman begged behind as we walked on. That lady cursed us there then by all that was holy and unholy above and below the sun.

We laughed. That lady, despite her cruel education could not understand that you could no longer curse the damned: you cannot curse the accursed.

We walked on. We were on coming home.

Every day we felt that we were getting nearer. We were arriving and our sins, they too, were coming home to roost. I carried my brother, but this brother carried our sins. His body, bloated and corrupted with all that we had done. His body, our bodies, was beyond being any burden, but we wondered how far we could walk and how far had we yet to come. Then one day, one day when strength and love and hate were no longer enough, we rounded a lone knoll and saw in the distance the purple foothills of the Hartz Mountains. We were home. This was our homeland. We had made it back at last.

Nothing remained above ground save the battered kirk and the blackened kirkyard. The rest might have been ruins or might have been nothing at all. We continued to lie to one another, saying here is Tante Erica's hus and here is the cripple Elisha's cobbling shop and over yonder the schoolhus.

Ding! Ding!

We stood awhile imitating the auld schoolmistress's ringing of the hand-bell. We recited mathematical tables, names of kings, queens and long dead emperors as well as half of a rhyme that functioned as a mnemonic of the colours of a rainbow. We laughed, cried a little, but finally moved on. Our schooling was over. There was nothing left for us to learn.

We kicked open the door of the kirk and a huge crossbeam crashed to the floor, disturbing dust but not us. The silence returned, no longer sacred just empty. We did not bend our knees nor genuflect. We staggered to a pew and lay down awhile to rest. There was dust. There was silence. There was not God. We lay on broken pews, rested, wept and wept again for all our sins and for our journey all but over.

Take, take anything you want, but don't torture me, said this voice. And we looked around. We even looked up at the debris covered Christ at the head of his kirk still nailed to his cross. But, it was no Christ. It was the village priest, creeping out from under the altar, dusting himself down, yet somehow managing to wring his hands in supplication. It was good to see him, but he could not help, not now. It was our parish priest, a gibbering wreck of a man, held together by a lang discredited catechism.

When the priest realised that we did not intend to kill, maim or torture him he volunteered to help my brother and me. He fetched or found old tools while we salvaged broken pews. We became hot as we worked, we sweated one last time: one last great offensive, one last push forward. While we worked the priest informed us what had gone on, the horror, oh the horror, of what had gone on in his own parish – what had been done. Everyone was dead or fled, everyone had gone except he - he had remained, he and his God. Waiting.

His chatter faltered when I laid my brother down in our homemade, makeshift coffin, when he saw my brother there his suspicions were at last aroused. The uniform had faded, but not quite enough. The priest started to whine, to complain, even to say the Lord God of Israel's name in vain, but I could not relent, not after all my brother and I had been through. The priest, this priest too, asked if it was all over. We were testimony. We were witnesses. We could not assure him. He continued to look ill at ease. We could no longer care. We made him harl the coffin to the kirkyard. We made him help as we dug the grave. He tried to question, but we were beyond all questioning. We were our own answers finally. We were brothers at last as I made him grant us extreme unction, knowing it was too late for us. The priest blubbed his words and we could not care. As he hammered down the lid he begged, he asked us then not to leave him alone. He said it was a sin, that we were putting his immortal soul in danger, but what was that to us. He even tried bribery, saying that he would teach us all his tricks: how to call down God in a glass of wine and a strip of bread, the power of naming over the newly born and how to take away the sins of the dead.

We told this man of a desert God to kneel down and pray for crows, for a black storm of ravens and clean summer snow. We told this man of the one true God to pray for this at least.

We did not say farewell.

Then this priest too cursed us as he flung down sod after sod over our coffin, as he tried to bury all thought of us.

That lone priest, we were beyond all that he had had or could now offer, beyond the living and the dead. We only asked for him not to mark our grave to tamp back the soil, quickly. Home, I whispered.

My brother and I we are home at last.

Holiday On Earth

A S Hopkins Hart

I

I realised I was different from everybody else when I heard
Thatcher and Gorbachov discussing nuclear politics under my
bed. It was a B&B in Blackpool and the landlady had let me
the room for £10 a night. There must have been a party
conference going on - why else would Mrs Thatcher be in the
same B&B as me?

Angela is my name and adventure is my spirit. I was baptised Angela in Portsmouth where my father was a sailor. Navy's rum was his downfall, but before he sailed off the edge, my mum gave birth to me. I was born a girl. As I lay in the cradle smiling she looked at me and thought how angelic I seemed. An Angel. A messenger from God.

So started an adventure that would spin ten million electrons (and span ten years.)

II

It began as quickly as it ended. With a bang. A big bang. It was the fuse blowing in the bedside lamp. I was inside that fuse feeling the warmth of millions of electrons.

Nigel, my blond electronics tutor, said to think of the electrons as cold, hungry tramps.

'Imagine a cold trainstation and a lovely kind tea-lady who puts hot mugs of tea on one end of the platform. On the other end are the cold, hungry tramps,' he told me. 'When a force is applied, the electrons move.'

The tea-lady was that force. Thus, I began my life as a result of ten million cold and hungry tramps rushing across a draughty train station because a kind tea-lady decided to make them all a nice cup of tea.

'I'll put the kettle on love, aren't you cold?' Mum says nowadays. She hardly ever mentions that blown fuse.

III

The next day I woke up and couldn't remember a thing. This often happened. Ten minutes of nagging doubt. Wasn't I a real star-traveller? But here's my story. You decide.

Her: Two pints of lager and a packet of nuts, please.

Me: (Struggling to stop the cap on my front tooth falling out)

Can I have lager in my lime, please?

Her: Have you got a sweet tooth?

Me: Only for you, darling.

Her: I hate people calling me darling.

Me: Oh. (crestfallen) Sorry.

We sat down in a corner without speaking.

Her: Oh, I've just seen someone I know...

This kind of thing was always happening to me.

IV

Handy Hints on Holiday or Tips for star-wanderers.

One of the good things about my ten year holiday here on Earth is money. You'd think after ten years you'd start running out of the odd dollar or two but the brilliant thing about earth is that getting money is simple.

I'll tell you.

All you do is go to one of earth's registered doctors and admit you are really a star-wanderer. The Earthling doctor won't believe you, they're so thick it's quite hilarious, and they will give you a piece of paper with 'psychotic' written on it. You take this to Earth's government health offices though and they think it's the last word in spiritual wisdom and start handing you money for it...Simple, isn't it?

'Calling all star-wanderers... Come to Earth for a ten-year holiday.'

V

An unusual feature of my home-star is the need for us to recharge our batteries. Don't get me wrong, the populations there aren't androids; in fact, they're a hundred times more human than humans, with a hundred times more warmth and emotions, too. When star-wanderers get depressed, they really go down on bumpy matter six foot below. And, when a star-wanderer is happy, she is on top of the galaxy.

Earthlings can't cope with star-wanderers, especially in, what Nigel tells me is called, the Northern Hemisphere. (England and the English are notorious for their 'stiff upper lip'.)

On my particular asteroid in the Southern Galaxy, just beyond the second black hole on the left, parallel in series to the Highlighter Natural Current of Electrons, Protons and Neutrons, people are more understanding.

Here in England you can drag yourself out of bed on a morning, half killing yourself with effort, stagger to the bus-stop or tube station nearly crying with pain, and some English person will look into your suicidal eyes and say,

'Nice day, innit, love.'

We star-wanderers just don't do that sort of thing.

VI

The noise, like an old-fashioned air-raid siren, penetrated everywhere, even into the nicotine-stained smoking room, the only place in this abandoned corner of the globe, where you were allowed to smoke.

Smoking. What a devastating habit. I'd picked it up when I'd first landed up here. Smoking was stopping me returning to my planet. The nicotine was fogging up the barcode on my astral travel-pass. I'd begin lift-off and couldn't even get through the ceiling. Universal Mission Control couldn't read me. I was stuck in this physical body and my cells wouldn't convert to astral. I kept crashing to the floor in a heap of dust.

Daniel, the morning domestic, came in with a mop and bucket.

'What's all this mess?' he demanded.

'Sorry, love, it's just my stardust,' I answered apologetically.

'More like fag-ash if you ask me. You lot live like animals.'

Daniel was bugging me. The noise was bugging me. It wouldn't stop. I thought it might be some poor miserable person being tortured, then realised all the alarms were going off.

Someone had escaped. It was me.

VII

The church was quiet and I wondered how much I would get for the candelabras. I had been on earth ten years today and I needed a drink. God, I was nearly twenty when I left my home-star, and was beginning to get a wee bit homesick. I wondered if my sister-species wife had borne a miniature Angelita yet.

Oh, Universal God of the Universe, the murder, the suspense of daughter-bearing. Why am I so far away when she's so close, so near, but so unattainable? If only I could stop smoking these damn cigarettes!

The nicotine had fogged up the barcodes completely now. When I tried my astral travel-pass it just went beep. What must I do to get free of the weed, quit this disgusting habit and abolish overflowing ashtrays? I've got to get back to my homestar in time for the birth of my baby, which me and my lover had conceived ten years ago in passionate embrace by sucking the wax out of each others ears. At least she won't have earache, I thought consolingly.

Will she press the baby-button and have the infant delivered or will she wait for my homecoming?

I heard a rustling noise behind me. Father Flanelegan came bursting out of the confessional box, saying, 'There's no drinking from the baptism font, my child.'

I stood up. My fringe was soaking wet. I lifted my hand to

try and rub it dry, but a packet of twenty Regal King Size fell out of my pocket into the holy water.

'And you can't smoke in church,' he added, in a gentle Irish accent.

VIII

Father Flanelegan.

His kind ginger eyes stared eagerly as he pointed to the confessional box.

'Have I got a customer?'

I didn't have the heart to tell him I was an atheist. I nodded my head and allowed myself to be directed into the confessional box. Once inside I looked round in amazement. It was an old converted astral-shuttle! I checked the controls. They were still intact. I didn't need my astral travel-pass any longer. This might just get me home.

I couldn't believe my luck. All I needed now were some decent clothes. I couldn't possibly turn up on my home-star in blue jeans and a Black Sabbath t-shirt on a seventies model astral-shuttle. I'd be the laughing stock of the neighbourhood. A space-robe would do the trick. I told Father Flanelegan how I'd been sleeping rough and offered him a donation to the church fund in return for his cassock. I dug deep in my pocket and pulled out all the earth-money I'd not used. There was about £2,200 in fifty-pound notes. His bottom jaw dropped as he stared at the collection plate: I thrust the throttle into first gear and managed to get lift off. He was still open-mouthed as the top of the confessional box blew up and hit the ceiling. His purple and gold cassock was flapping in the air above his head. 'Jesus, Mary and Joseph' were the last words I heard him utter. I will never forget them.

IX

The astral-shuttle flew about the church, lurching from side to side. I clung on for dear life. As soon as there was enough power I jammed onto the frequency of Universal Mission Control and screamed at the mike.

'Get me out of here! Beam me up, Lotty!'

A sister-species star-wanderer's harmonic voice broke the silence. They'd heard me. I revved up the engine. The exhaust bellowed out a cloud of smoke which set all the bells in the belfry clanging. The noise was like an aggravated version of the alarms I'd heard when I'd escaped from that terrible institution. I looked down at the ground. A red-faced woman was screaming,

'Get her down from there.'

I could hear a van screeching to a halt outside. I revved the engine again and jammed the throttle on full. I had to get away. The exhaust spluttered out star-fumes, then a blast blew me through the roof, extinguishing all the candles on the altar. I had lift-off. I put the shuttle onto auto-pilot and lit up a fag.

X

'Gas fumes,' the man from Transco Gas Co explained.

'You're lucky to be alive,' he added and stared up at the heavens.

Later, I heard that Father Flanelegan had been seen putting up a sign which read 'Church Roof Fund - All donations gratefully received'

XI

I locked into star-space and docked on a hillside on my home-star, not far from where I lived. I didn't want to park too close in case Mrs Beady Eye at No 23 was watching. They'd all be twitching their net curtains as it was.

I climbed out of the cabin and looked at my watch. Twenty minutes. Not bad for a seventies-style astral shuttle. I started downhill, going faster with each stride. The grass felt like sponge under my feet. The view unfolded before me. I'd not forgotten how beautiful it was. When I got to the end of our street, I thought I could see what looked like a flag. I got closer. There was no need for a yellow ribbon. The forty white nappies flapping on the line said it all. Twins. We call them Angelita and Angelina. Lita and Lina for short. When they grow up they want to be star-wanderers. I know they'll be good at it. It's in their blood.

Mind Creatures

Chris Firth

My calling here would be my doom, I knew, but I could not resist my old friend's plea. Thus, at the appointed time I arrived before the door of 7 Rosechester Grove and rapped hard upon the polished oak. The curving, tree-lined street disturbed me with its bland normality - regularly spaced, three floored, detached abodes, shaped in squares of clean sandstone blocks, fronted by narrow strips of lawned gardens. Each house seemed identical to the next but for some minor detail of curtain colour or garden plant arrangement. Around me, that calm, suburban street shimmered like a fragile desert mirage.

Delay in answer to my knocking seemed inevitable, for it was well known to family and friends that Otto Loxley had become something of a recluse. He shunned contact with the outside world, rarely received visitors, and had not emerged from his house for over three years. My own summons there had been completely psychic - flashes of the house front in frantic nightmares, and the half-whispered voice of Loxley sounding in the depths of my brain. He begged me to come, uttering directions to me when it seemed that I had lost track of my destination. I had no physical invitation - no card or letter - requesting my visit.

I knew that he had married, but of his wife I knew nothing. As I had become a 'nomadic wanderer' since last in Loxley's presence, my appearance was anything but decent, nor even exotic. I stank, and was filthy. Not expecting the warmest of welcomes, I would have retreated then, had not something fluttered, soft as moths' wings, beyond the door. A tiny glass peephole was fitted into the wood. I prickled uncomfortably, aware that through the lens somebody was studying me. Anxious neighbours were probably peering from behind window blinds, wondering why some vagrant had come to sully the serenity of their street.

Waiting for this uncomfortable sense of scrutinisation to pass, I shifted too and fro on the flags of the porch, tapping the toes of my withered shoes upon the stones. Eventually a latch clicked. The door swung inward. A young woman loomed in the half-opened doorway, pale-skinned, blonde hair, utterly beautiful. She calmly surveyed my face, her eyes dazzling pools of bright blue mist. She was very tall, slender-necked, gleaming hair hanging to her shoulders in a crisply cut bob. She reminded me of a swan I had seen gliding upon a lake one summer at twilight. Apart from a slim band of wedding ring and a fine golden chain around her wrist she was without ornament, even her face devoid of make-up.

'So it is you…' Her dry voice had a crisp, piano neatness. She peered directly into my eyes, then retracted, as if slightly disappointed.

'I'm Hannah, Otto's wife,' she clipped. 'We've been expecting you. Come in.'

She stepped back without handshake or any indication of intimacy. I followed her through a fragrant wake of light perfume, noticing the fine cut of her grey two piece suit. So assured and sophisticated in appearance and manner, she seemed the very antithesis of me. I felt gross in her presence, as though exposed to my rotten core. There I was, meat and beer bloated in my ragged black clothes and tatty beard, reeking of the street. I, who had roamed homeless for years with my writhing emptiness and sense of misplacement. Shuffling and stinking behind this slim, delicate creature, she led me along the corridor of her home. She even trod with the light foot-fall and the easy, fluid steps of a ballet dancer. I stumbled behind her - a hippopotamus trailing a gazelle. She was so complete and accomplished, yet for all my flaws and ragged edges she seemed to accept me without prejudice or question. How had Loxley been so fortunate? While I roamed the world, he had located himself in this comfortable house, with a beautiful wife who loved him, who tolerated his eccentricities, and who appreciated his capacity for the spiritual.

Hannah showed me into a spacious room that, like herself, was absent of fuss or clutter. To our left was a large bay window, the glass panes covered with white paper blinds, just enough light filtering through to create a relaxing luminosity. All surfaces - a low table, shelves, fireplace, walls and ceiling - were either stripped and bleached wood, or painted white, even the polished floor boards long, single planks of white Scandinavian pine. I felt as though I had walked into the inside of a Chinese paper lantern. The room's only touch of colour was a single, brilliant-blue and flame-yellow iris, trumpeted fully open, dazzling there in a long-necked white vase upon the oval table. This startling decor seemed very 'eastern', a simple purity of line and surface that an interior design brochure might term 'nouveau Zen.' So typical of Loxley, of whom, decor aside, there was no sign.

'He resides in the attic these days,' Hannah explained, as if somehow aware of my line of thought.

'I'll inform him that you've arrived in a moment, but first...' She waved me to a curved bench that ran like an eyebrow along the edge of the table. '...I'm sure you'd like to take tea.'

This was a statement, not an invitation. As I sat down she vanished through a corner door, leaving me feeling self-conscious and grimy, a gross contamination of the place. There was nothing to do but stare upon that beautiful iris and contemplate the harmony of the room. A cat, a fluffy white Persian, lay curled in sleep before the unlit fireplace. To entertain myself I made the appropriate gum-clicks and hissing noises, attempting to gain its attention, but it did not stir. I would have risen and poked at it, but Hannah returned then, gliding in with a silver tea-tray, which she set upon the table. Over tea - inevitably prepared with much ritual and attention to detail - we discussed her husband. In particular she talked about his difficulty of reintegrating himself into normal society after his years of seclusion and meditation. Apparently this problem, and my opinion upon it, was the reason for my presence there. She spoke openly, aware that I was familiar with the robust, sociable Loxley of old.

'Of course you know he spent many years out east,' she sighed, as though this subject was tiresome to her. 'He set off from Australia in a boat he built. Lived in Japan a while, then travelled through China, toTibet, then moved out to Mustang.'

'Ah, yes,' I nodded, just for the sake of agreeing. Her own voice suddenly lilted with enthusiasm.

'But of course, you'll know all about Mustang. That's where Otto first came across you.'

Her statement surprised me. My own recollections of that time were hazy, half-formed, for I had travelled far and changed a great deal since then.

'I believe so,' I murmured, my eyes gazing off as I struggled up buried memories. Mountainscapes with vast, cloud-peppered skies; rock-hewn towns and citadels hand carved into perilous cliff-tops; huge, underground caverns illuminated by thousands of white candles, with row upon row of saffron-robed monks, scalps gleaming, sitting erect while chanting hypnotic mantras. And there amidst them I saw again the shaven head and long, goatish face of Loxley. He loomed and bobbled before me, eyes closed, a gentle smile sealed upon his blood-red lips.

'We studied there,' I remembered aloud, blinking away the vision. 'With ancient Lamas.'

'Yes, so Otto says.'

'We studied the works of the Buddha and other Bodhisattvas.'

'It's here where he became intrigued with his production of *Tulpa.*'

'*Tulpa?*' I repeated, not understanding the word.

'Yes. Imaginative Matter, he says, though I don't think there is a literal translation. I think that his experiments began there, though you'd know more about that than me.'

I sat there, obviously looking perplexed, for she went on impatiently.

'You know, making ideas within the mind become actual *things*. Things in the world of matter. *Yang-tul, Nying-tul.* Those things.'

I struggled with this twist in the conversation, those Tibetan phrases ringing with a vague familiarity, but making me feel uneasy.

'You mean making dreams come true?' I ventured.

'No, no, not dreams. Not just dreams. They're too chaotic. They lack shape and solid edges. Ideas, I'm talking about. Real ideas. Mental forms.'

Silence blossomed between us, and there was a delicate fiddling of tea cups while she struggled for the words to explain, and me for the knowledge to understand.

'Well, anyway, not just that,' she said. 'I did think that you'd be familiar with his creations. What do I call them? English has nothing.'

'Mind-creatures,' I offered, recalling a conversation I'd had with Loxley while travelling down through the mountains from Mustang to Nepal.

'Yes. Those. Mind-creatures.'

'But it always seemed so absurd.'

Her eyebrows arched surprise, the first real feeling I had seen in her impassive face.

'You never believed in Otto then?'

My mind wandered back to memories of Mustang - the fantastic feats of mind and body I had witnessed - that had been achieved by monks after years of study and isolated meditation. Those priests who had defied gravity and hovered in sustained levitation above the ground. The monk's cell that we had broken open after his designated period of fasting and meditation - we had found him cross-legged and motionless, peacefully blissful on some other spiritual or mental plain, eyes closed, face radiant. Such a look of serenity upon his face, yet the flesh of his right hand and forearm eaten away by black ants which still swarmed upon the bone. As I drifted over these memories Hannah rose, summoning me to follow.

'Well then, before we go up to the attic, I'd best familiarise you.'

She led me toward a corner where a pine panel slid back to reveal a door, which she pushed open. A stone staircase led down into gloom and darkness.

'The basement,' she explained. 'The light switch is just there, beyond the door.'

She stepped back to allow me room to pass her without touching.

'You'll be quite safe. These are just early experiments. I barely even notice them anymore. It may be that you won't even see anything - the people who come to check the meters never seem to.'

I stepped through, pressed on the light, and began the descent, my footsteps ringing into the hollow. I had little idea of what awaited me down there; no real clue from what Hannah Loxley had been saying.

The cellar was dry and airy - a huge whitewashed rectangle with a clean floor of sandstone flags. The place was empty except for the gas and electricity meters which were set side by side in the far wall, staring across like a great pair of mechanical eyes. A door arch led into an area of darkness directly opposite the foot of the stairs - the old coal-hole, common in these older types of houses, or so I presumed. My feet clacked onto the stone flags, and I swivelled to glance back up at the silhouette of Hannah Loxley, wondering why she had sent me down here. Fear and suspicion preyed at my mind. Perhaps this enchanting woman was not quite as civilised as she seemed, and this was all a ploy - part of some sinister trick to entomb me there in the basement, for whatever dark intentions.

'Don't be afraid - they can't harm you," she called down. 'Around you - on the ground...'

I saw them then all right, scattered over the floor, scrabbling hungrily toward my feet. Crudely formed, shapeless things, most of them about the size of a fat mouse - shimmering, blue-grey blobs of sparkling slime that seemed to glide without friction just above the surface of the floor. Despite their ease of movement they were slow, taking several seconds to reduce their pace or change direction, thus I had no difficulty in stepping out of their way. Fascinated, I gazed upon them, and the more definite, concentrated ones began to take on shapes, as if their fluid bodies were filling invisible moulds. Stumps of limbs formed before my gaze, jellied tentacles groping out of globes of heads, large, embryonic eyes glazing hard upon liquid miniature faces. They looked much like anemones and gastropods from the dark green depths of some ancient ocean.

'You see them, then?' Hannah Loxley called down as she watched me pick my way across the floor, trying to avoid treading on the things.

'They're quite harmless,' she reassured. 'They're free of malice.'

'Now listen here,' I barked, sounding far braver than I felt. 'These things are nothing. They're just trickery. They don't frighten me, if that's what you're intention is.'

'No, no,' she said. 'I'm sorry if that's what it seems like. Look, come on up now. We'll go and see Otto. I'm sure he'll explain everything.'

But I was in no hurry to go up the stairs. More of the miraculous creatures were streaming from the darkened archway across the cellar, all swarming in a determined line toward my ankles. Nebulous forms shimmered, vanished, then reappeared again within seconds, as if slipping in and out of time, struggling to maintain themselves within this reality. At times they crowded too close upon each other and bodies merged, new limbs, tails and tendril-horns sprouting upon the

172

fresh surface. On my way back toward the staircase I cruelly stepped upon some of the 'creatures' as an experiment, wondering at their capacity to feel and respond to pain. They melted away from the pressure of my shoe like liquid mercury, the scattered globules reforming themselves into renewed, animate forms once clear of my footfall.

Eventually, I returned to the room above and closed the basement door. Hannah, barely able to contain a triumphant smile, was waiting for me, framed across in the doorway to the entrance lobby.

'What you just saw are the earliest efforts of Otto's meditations,' she explained. 'But come now, we'll go up. You can meet him again yourself.'

'The cat,' I said, warily eyeing the creature as I crossed the room. Even as I spoke it moved, lazily rolling in on itself, inverting, legs passing through its own insubstantial body to emerge on the other side. The thing stood up then, lowering its forelegs and pushing down to stretch its back. Also 'imaginary', it gazed up at me with smoky, half-formed eyes.

'Beautiful, isn't she?' Hannah crooned. 'I couldn't bear to banish her to the cellar with the others. Such a shame about the eyes though. Eyes are always such a problem for Otto.'

The cat floated up, billowing cloud-like ahead of us along the hallway. We stepped into a large, gloomy space that seemed like a cave after the white brightness of the lounge. This new room, at the core of the house, was empty but for the base of an elaborately cast, wrought-iron staircase. The black steps and railings were decorated with a fine motif of ivy leaves and budding roses. Looking upward from the bottom step I could see that this staircase went coiling away with the delicate artistry of a spider's web, spiralling up through a series of floors, tapering to some distant vanishing point that must have been at least five stories beyond the ground floor where we stood - something not physically possible within the confined dimensions of the house that I had seen from the outside.

'This way now,' Hannah said softly, touching me for the first time, taking my left arm and leading me onto the bottom step. The cat remained there at the foot of the staircase, its nebulous eyes staring after us as we began the ascent.

'Don't fear anything we might meet along the way,' Hannah whispered. Her breath buzzed soft and warm against my ear, my bestial stomach churning at the overwhelming notion that this lovely woman might be about to kiss and seduce me. She took my quivering hand in hers, her touch warm silk, leading me as if I was a frightened child.

'Try to keep your other hand on the stair-rail, unless I tell you otherwise. Everything you'll meet is harmless, really. You'll simply witness more evolved versions of those ideas that you saw there in the basement.'

I was led upward. Time seemed to slow and blur, movements and words jerking then slurring, every fraction of sound or motion edged and separated like a film frame. Each moment became a droplet, an independent bead, not relying on those before or after for meaning. The flow of time itself was halting. My thoughts could not form properly, every portion of each thought fragmenting, pixelating at the edges, fanning out into other possibilities. Every moment became a doorway into an infinite potentiality of others. This startling, labyrinthine confusion had my head pulsating with pain, as though my brain was about to explode out of my skull. I faltered, groaning, gripping at my temples with one hand, nauseous, in agony. Hannah shushed and cooed at my shoulder, attempting to calm and comfort me.

'Don't worry, this confusion soon passes. Come on now...'

Her feather-soft fingers wove between mine, and she tugged at my hand. I staggered on. Like this, like a mother leading her injured child, we climbed up into rooms where it was as if a veil had at last been torn from before my eyes. Solid walls shimmered, fading, becoming non-existent as a series of landscapes opened up around us. Deep, wooded valleys and rocky plains uncurled visibly, as if we were standing within the stamen of some incredible flower, the petals of which were unfolding into bright sunshine, each petal painted with living detail of an astounding view. Dense green jungles, carpeted with flowers, stretched away toward ranges of violet mountains. Tiny birds of pure, pulsating light, like condensed rainbows, flitted around the fruit-crowded branches of enormous baobab trees. If ever there had ever been a Paradise, then it was here. I yearned to step from the staircase and explore these astonishing places, but when I moved to do so Hannah squeezed my hand, tugging me back as easily as if I had been a balloon.

'Not yet,' she insisted. 'You don't want to leave the staircase just yet. You'd only go adrift out there, and there's so much more to see.'

As we ascended to the next floor a unicorn came dazzling out of a hazel thicket like a streak of white lightning. Snorting fiercely, slashing its deadly razor-horn, it bolted at us, yellow eyes ablaze with rage. I would have fled this ferocity but Hannah stood there firmly, simply smiling upon the creature. Beneath her unwavering gaze it slowed and faltered. As if suddenly sapped of all fury, it trotted up, rolling to lay meekly on the ground before her.

'You may touch him, if you like,' she told me.

I reached down and stroked the smooth muzzle, then tentatively fingered the coralesque coils of horn. Suspecting illusion, I expected the creature to vanish upon contact with my fingers, but there it remained, solid, quivering, allowing me to run my hands over its head and hot back. Looking beyond the unicorn, I saw that the whole landscape here - terraced greenery descending to scattered lakes and rock-pools - was teeming with other incredible creatures, all moulded from myth and fantasy. Around the shore of the nearest lake, basking lazily upon ochre sands and within the emerald shallows, lay huge, frog-legged creatures with shelled tortoise bodies, but each with the chattering head of a chimpanzee. Kangaroo-legged marsupials with tiny, leathered wings and the heads of grinning lizards hopped leisurely in the undergrowth. Twittering away, perched there in the lower branches of nearby trees, were rows of griffins and horned, dog-headed birds.

'Fantastic...' was the only, mundane utterance I was capable of, my small voice so ridiculous amidst those scenes around us. Startled at the sound, the unicorn leapt up and blurred away between the trees. It's panic set the other creatures astir. Swinging down from the treetops, snarling and full of menace, came grotesque, red-winged apes, their limbs and torsos anthropoid, but with the heads and hind talons of golden eagles. Hannah yanked at my hand and we continued climbing, accompanied now by a swarm of flying serpents. They hovered around us with blurring wings, white fangs ominously bared, tiny tongues rasping in and out.

'Step off when he's not ready and you could become meshed in with the ideas, or tangled into the scenery,' Hannah whispered. 'As long as we stay on the staircase they are harmless.'

'Yes, yes,' I nodded, understanding some of it now. 'They must be harmless. One man alone could not create such illusions.'

'Hardly illusions!' She laughed at the very notion. 'You touched it, that unicorn. You felt it. Matter. Completely independent of his mind now. To be fair though, it does take a receptive intelligence to recreate his projections. He compares the process to television. Specific equipment is needed to pick up transmitted signals, then decode them into sounds and pictures. Without a receiver the images don't really exist, do they? Just invisible signals and waves flittering away into a void.'

'It's ridiculous!' I shook my head, trying to clear it of her voice and the hallucinations around me. 'None of this is possible here.'

'Shush, now.' Hannah raised a finger against her lips. 'Sudden noise may harm him if he's in deep meditation. It's best to recall him gently.'

We stepped from the staircase into a cottage garden, crazy-stone paths leading away between beds of ornamental flowers and kitchen herbs. The air around us was thick-scented, alive with birdsong and insect-drone. She led me along a shaded ash grove to where a path ended at a gateway, its green planks set within a brick wall. A silver handbell rested upon a mossy boulder, and this she gathered up, ensuring that her fingers enclosed the stopper to prevent any accidental ringing. Three times, gently and with ritualistic care, she rang that bell. As the last chime faded toward silence that world of life and colour dissolved to white mist, the horizons spinning inward, folding on each other in a kaleidoscopic spiral of light. The red wall and the planks of the gateway also melted. At last, we stepped through into Otto Loxley's attic retreat.

Far from the tidy, minimal cell I had expected, the room was littered with dismantled electronic equipment, broken fragments of porcelain, glass beads, marbles, tiny shards of bright plastic, loose coils of copper wire. There seemed no order to this chaos of junk and components - none of it seemed to be wired up or connected to an energy source. Mote-filled sunbeams poured through a skylight in the steep angled ceiling. There, on the plank floor, surrounded by more of this wiring and cluttered circuitry, basking in those rays of sunshine, sat Loxley. His back was rigid, and he was cross-legged in the lotus-posture of meditation. He was naked, a whisping moustache and beard coiling down onto his chest. So odd looking, yet so familiar. Those absurd brushes of eyebrows, the finely ridged ivory brow and hollowed cheeks, ringlets of unkempt grey hair cascading down around his bony shoulders.

'He's here,' Hannah crooned. She sounded soft and distant now, as if her voice was muffled by clouds of cotton wool.

His nostrils flared, chest heaving as he inhaled a slow breath until the ribs stood out like a bare rack. Eyes snapped open, blazing onto mine. The goatish pupils were startling and disturbing, each merely a horizontal smear of cloudy violet. Trembling with awe, I held that terrible gaze, and it was then that I knew for sure. Those eyes of golden mist. That face. Otto Loxley. Myself. One living being stared upon the replica of the other. As I frowned he frowned. When he smiled so did I. Each facial movement - a slight raising of the eyebrow, a quick pursing of the lips - was mimicked precisely, as if we were looking into a mirror without frame. He rose to greet me, face aglow with rapture, the genius mind pinning me there, forcing me to reciprocate the same loving ecstasy as, at last, we embraced. Images came spinning into my mind. A unicorn. A staircase. A fading rainbow. A single iris in a white vase. Each picture came sliding over the next like a shuffled pack of face-up playing cards. Hannah was speaking, her voice just tinkling from so far away now that I could not even decipher the words. Face to face with Otto, he pressed his brow upon mine, and I jolted, electrified, flashes of a world exploding, unfurling into my own mind. A vast, teeming world of events that I had never known. A stream of people that I had never met. A gallery of places that I could not have seen. My mind was erupting with memories that were not truly mine. Otto Loxley, still clasping me in that loving embrace, was filling me with himself. And as he did this, so even my gross body altered to become a replica of his, the folds of flesh and cellulite dissolving away, the scabs and sores of rough-living healing, melting away as he reshaped me.

Though I wanted to leave him then, though I wanted to tear away and be free to roam the chaotic corridors and mazes of this world I was glimpsing through his mind, I knew, with an overwhelming sense of dread, that it was never to be. As his creation, his *Tulpa,* it was my destiny to remain in the attic there - to stay forever within him while he went away. He was to explore; my duty and purpose was to remain there embalmed in meditation and thus sustain all this - all that he had created. I would never again feel spring rains patter upon my face, nor sense the autumn winds caress through my own hair. It would never be me who would close my eyes against the trees and sunshine of a real day, watching the light patterns dance there against the warmed, red lids.

His *Tulpa.* His play-thing. A creature to be the prisoner of his imagination.

Otto was crying then - we were crying together.

A tear each from our dazzling, amber, all-seeing eye.

Just Another Day

Sandra Bolas

Six o'clock silence, so different from the smoky tranquillity of evening. But guaranteed, at five past six the cars began to drone, spluttering and snoring, along the road. Soon, other noises filtered through the blinds, sharp glassy sounds. Another day…

In days gone by, she had imagined the gates of Heaven to say 'Marks and Spencer', and the rewards of absolution to be an unlimited credit card. The anticipation of lemon cheesecake and a new pair of knickers could really brighten the day. Today though, she was not in the mood for light entertainment. Closing her eyes as she passed the full length mirror, she remembered that there had been a time when the mirror had given pleasure and excitement; a long time ago now. Alone still, she realised the fear in freedom – kind of weightless and unanchored.

Downstairs, the house was cool. She felt the polished floor hard against her feet, spreading her toes in celebration – and then an explosion of glass from the kitchen door. Thousands of sharp slivers surrounded him. His feet were bare, like hers, but browner and wider; that was the first thing she noticed. Uncurling her body, she saw he was completely naked, and completely still. He stood there and stared for a while before his misty gaze drifted. Then seating himself at the table, his buttocks made a small slapping sound and she tried not to laugh.

He walked around the downstairs rooms, which all connected, slowly pacing the route – echoing the child she had once been, counting steps and pretending blindness. She watched as he discovered the brush and swept the glass shards into a heap. Maybe only lonely people learn to enjoy the sound of a soft brush on a wooden floor, the sound of splitting wood as a screw turned. Apprenticed to the art of listening, she smiled. In her dressing gown, she went to the shed and retrieved the piece of hardboard used when she had lost her keys and had to do a breaking and entering job on the back door. The board clicked into the grooves where the glass had been; it sounded like biscuits breaking.

Back at the table where he rested, she helped to pick the

glass out of his bleeding hands, arranging the shards in a row along the striped tablecloth. His body gave out a kind of shine, not bright, but a glow like the embers of a bonfire. Enclosed like this, she needed nothing.

On other uncounted, discounted days of boredom she had planned her escape route carefully – what to do when fire descended, or the mad rapist came to call. Funny now, but she made no attempts to run.

She lifted her hands to his face. Slowly stroking, his skin felt like cool burned woodash, hardly there at all, and when she released his body it left a shadow on hers. Who knows what she really felt? Excitement, or maybe guilt, like finding a wallet belonging to someone else. All the while knowing you ought to hand it in, but you delay it a couple of hours to spend money imaginatively for once.

He was full of shadows, hollows where she had only flesh. She took his hand, an intertwining of feather-soft fingers, and led him to the bedroom. Laying down beside him, she waited while he took the knife and slowly moved it first across hers, and then his own throat. As time stood still, she closed her eyes and dreamt of childhood. This dream was full of colours that burned like fire and tasted of grass and oranges. Each flake of snow had six points and was unique. The fireworks were stars. She heard the flowers breath as the bloody sun sank slowly down.

Tree

Liz Hoyle

She'd flown through the tunnel to light - that light which still bedazzles those who've glimpsed it through death. She'd felt nothing when the infinitesimal clump of particles broke from her fading brain; a scintilla of consciousness freed to travel randomly, swifter than light, than time, surpassing space. That scintilla of self was now her self all over again in micro-time - not in crumbling memories, but life, her life, wound back faster than times she had lived: from the rising sear of flesh and flaming paint-on-steel-and-petrol and the screaming tyres and her man, until the dwindling, veined, translucent girl, herself, unborn. It was all the pain, fun, blushing humdrum play of life enacted for the first time. Then the blood-red curtain rose.

What stage was this? Was she now before herself, unborn? She wasn't aware that a particular scrap of her self had slipped through a leakage, a 'worm-hole', worm-holed into the laws of another universe. She was not aware that the tunnel had been micro-dimensional; she'd lost count of dimensions, not sensed herself stretched, flicked back into alternate space. Throughout all Times of all Universes come and gone, her survival was unique, being the first to come through Nothingness while recognising nothing.

'Am I dead?' she wondered. Bodiless and headless, yet sentient. She tried resolving that, tried making sense of smelling of what she saw, of hearing smells, of seeing sounds through no bony cavities. Denied sinus for feeding of faeces, she was emptiness. Having no skin, she knew no boundaries, and failed to get the measure of her self. Then she remembered her name. Me-a. 'Mia!'

She drifted then, trying to make sense of this dim light. She moved among strange colours, vibrant but cold. Yesterday, she might have wondered if these were the shades bees saw in white daisies and cloud-tops and frosts. Here were no reds, no corals, nor ambers, no colours of roses. There were acids, blues and ultra-blues reflected in quick-silverish unwetting pools. Mia feared this Heaven Hell as she drifted against rough blocks, as draughts swirled her around and between metallic poles that rose from plains of dark, dense gas. The light lowered as lichen-clouds muffled the sky, then throbbed and shook until everything fibrillated ochre sounds and fluttered musks. Something was pushing warmth toward her - something smelling of egg-yolk, purposeful, alive! It paused, and air around it rippled silently like an enveloping life-pond, rippling the egg-smell, rippling waves of 'What are you?' to Mia.

She responded: 'I am... not You, I - I am Mia.'

For a while, everywhere was dull and cool, and Mia inwardly wailed.

'Is Mia alone? Show me You - show me You, here!'

Suddenly the egg-smell spun, took shape, forming a stem that grew looming translucence over her, scattering light-dust and the word 'Observe!'

Mia did observe as it flickered and stood tree-like, not solid but as clusters of sparkles streaming along pathways like cells in a vein. The pathways branched out, blossoming sequins, trembling lilacs and piccolo notes.

'Now you see us as many and one!'

And Mia became many as she too fragmented. Her invisible branches leaned toward You, grew around You - and recoiled, shrivelling and singed. The You Tree was burning. It burnt acid green, the smoke dripping odours of scorched aluminium, scattering hot sequins stinging the gas-ground. The Tree was seeding itself. Mia flew like the child she had been, the child who once leapt for falling leaves. Mia moved among sequins, catching them, attaching them, defining the edges and ends of her linear self. She sparkled, grew rooted and flourished.

Time passed until transcendent Mia vibrated, again shaking off her own hot seeds.

Pondlife...

Julie Mellor is from Penistone and lives in Sheffield. She graduated from the University of Huddersfield in 1996, and has completed an MA in creative writing at Sheffield Hallam. She has had a few short stories published, including one in *London Magazine* and in Route's ***Tubthumping*** collection. She has also completed a novel, *Life Without Mirrors*.

Rose Hughes is from Liverpool and lives in Leeds. ***Velvet Swamp*** was first published in *Metropolitan* Magazine. She has written plays and short stories, and co-ordinated an oral history publication. Rose has taught creative writing in Leeds. Her latest literary adventure is a fanzine: *The Gobshite*.

Zenko Zdolyny is of Ukranian origin and lives in Bradford with his wife and two children. He plays trombone and the accordion and has toured as a musician with various bands. He now co-runs a joint owned company, Visual Blinds, and writes crime and horror fiction whenever he can find the time. He writes mainly screen-plays but as yet his work is not available on celluloid. This is his first published short story.

Neil Benbow hides in the trees and caves of South Devon with his family. Having nothing at all to do with 'the north', he is the yin in our yang. He had two stories published in ***Tubthumping*** (Route). Apart from the fact that he lives in a place called Happy Valley, and is a prolific writer of short stories, very little is known about him. A complete recluse, he is allegedly attempting to grow his toe-nails to a world record length.

John Barfoot completed the MA in Creative Writing at Northumbria University. He is a mild mannered civil servant, by day. By night he roams the streets of Newcastle and verbally abuses hapless tourists at cash dispensers. He has written many stories over several years, and is a published writer of science fiction stories. You may have seen him on *Crimewatch*.

Simon Crump is from Loughborough, but has lived in Sheffield for twenty years. Like most people who have lived there for that long, he once briefly played with the band *Pulp*. He had a collection of short stories published by *Clocktower* in 1998, and in November 2000 Bloomsbury are publishing a collection of his short stories about Elvis Presley, *'My Elvis'*

Stephen Wade lives in Scunthorpe. He co-ordinates and teaches creative writing at the University of Huddersfield. He writes poetry and short stories. His most recent publication was a poetry collaboration with Tony Smith, performed at the Hull Literature Festival, and published by Stone Creek Press. This is his first published short story. He is currently editing a book on the history of Liverpool Poetry from the 60s until the present day, which includes contributions from Brian Patten and Roger McGough.

C. John Roberts lives in Thornton on the outskirts of Bradford, but his roots are in the tourist riddled and hollow hills of the Peak District. He graduated from the University of Bradford and is now a graphic designer. He says he has been writing since childhood and hopes to continue until the humming voices in his head are dead. He is working on a collection of cross genre short stories, which he hopes will be of interest to someone. *The Cold* is his first published short story.

Steven Mawson lives in Rotherham. He is a twenty-one year old writer of numerous unpublished short stories, mostly of a bizarre and macabre nature. He has a love of 'the twist' in fiction, and sees his short works as 'quick fix stories for lovers of compelling reading'. This is his first published short story. He is currently working on his first novel, for which he is seeking an agent or publisher.

S.M. Vickerman has resided in four continents but is now writing poetry and short stories as well as a novel, in the bleak Bronte hills to the north-west of Bradford. Virago Press published a story in their 1999 *Wild Cards* anthology, and *Diamond Twig Press* published poems in their *The Blue Room* anthology. Feature articles have also been written for *The Guardian* and the *TES* while working as a freelance journalist.

Sitara Khan lives and works in Leeds. Trentham Books recently published her book *A Glimpse Through Purdah: Asian Women, Myth and Reality*. She has a collection of short stories, from which Serpent emerges, for which she is seeking a publisher. She is currently working on her first novel.

Sue Wood has taught at universities in Australia and South Africa, and has had poetry published in both countries. She started writing short stories two years ago after being made 'redundant' from a FE College in Yorkshire. Her first short story was a runner-up in the Ian St James Award, she had a short story published in *Tubthumping* (Route), a story in *The New Writer* and one in the recently published *Neonlit: Time Out Book of New Writing*. She now writes, does the gardening and runs a bed and breakfast establishment in Halifax.

Ian Cusack lives in Newcastle. He was 'opted out' of teaching after a bullying Headteacher leapt onto the end of his wrath. He now writes as a freelance music and football journalist, as well as working on creative pieces. His poetry and short stories have been published in various literary magazines. Ian completed a Creative Writing MA at the University of Northumbria last year. A dedicated follower of Newcastle United, he attempts to compensate for this character flaw by drinking vast amounts of alcohol. He is presently teaching EFL in Slovakia.

Sue Wilsea lives in Hull. She used to be the editor for *Inkshed*, a long deceased northern magazine. She had short stories published in the past, but then managed to kick the writing habit, for a while. Despite acupuncture, hypnosis and experimentation with essential oils she has taken to writing again, and this is her first published story for quite some time.

Mandy MacFarlane is a Scottish/Sudanese writer from Dundee, now living in Leeds. Her writing has been published in *Cutting Teeth*, a Glasgow based magazine. She has written a collection of short stories and several screen plays. She is currently working on a screenplay. She is hoping to visit Khartoum, her father's 'home town', in the near future.

Daithidh MacEochaidh has been around a fair bit but lives in York. He has won a number of short story competitions, has had stories in Stand magazine, and had a story in Route's ***Tubthumping*** collection. Route are also publishing his first novel - ***Like A Dog To Its Vomit*** - in 2000 - a unique hyper-textual reading adventure that deconstructs post-modernism and back again.

A.S. Hopkins Hart lives in Leeds. She has had poetry and fiction published in American magazines, but this is her first British fiction to appear in print. She had a short collection of poetry, *Diary Of A Schizophrenic,* published by LSP Press, Leeds. She has written a collection of short stories for which she is seeking a publisher.

Chris Firth is from Bradford and lives in Whitby. He has had several short stories published, including one in **Tubthumping**. As Molly Firth, he has had **Electraglade** stories in *Quality Womens Fiction, Aquarius Women* and *Metropolitan.* His cult novel **Miasma** was published by Route in 1997. He has a collection of 'bizarre short fiction', **Hocus Pocus, Hullabaloo**, to be published by Solomon Press in April 2000. Samples of his **Electraglade** short story collection can be found at www.openingline.co.uk

Sandra Bolas lives in Dewsbury. She feels that she is lucky as a writer, having had five poems and a short story published after only starting to submit her work this year. She has just finished a degree in English, and now works teaching basic skills to people who are long-term unemployed. She has two children, and would love to have the freedom to write full time. She would also love to write a 'happy' story - but doesn't write well when she fells happy!

Liz Hoyle lives in Keighley. She was a teacher of audiology, working with deaf children for many years in Doncaster and Bradford. She retired three years ago due to ill health. Through work with Amnesty International, she is now a co-ordinator for *Lifelines,* setting up penfriend correspondence between British prisoners and USA inmates awaiting execution on Death Row. Later this year she is setting up a correspondence

Poetry Workshop for people in British prisons. She is 'housebound' due to her ill health, but now travels inward, exploring 'vast internal mindscapes' of which *'Tree'* is but a glimpse.